My Secret Master

A Dark Billionaire Romance

USA TODAY Bestselling Author

Nora Flite

Copyright © 2015 Nora Flite

ISBN-13: 978-1514749241

ISBN-10: 1514749246

- Chapter One -
Naomi

A preview of my future...

"You think you're not a slave, that you're not meant to kneel and please your Master." He chuckled, a noise that stroked my inner thighs as good as his hand could have. "I'll have fun proving you wrong."

Bending down, he caught my ankles. Easily, he spread them wide, fixing them inside two straps bolted to the floor.

Oh god, oh god! My chest was threatening to split open from the tremor in my lungs. I thought I'd been too deep before, but now, I knew what deep really meant.

"I'm going to break you," he whispered, circling behind me.

His voice coerced a wave of excitement. Determined to bury it, I stared at the far wall, but it was torture of another kind, because I could see the exit. I tugged at the ropes, knowing it was hopeless. *I'm trapped, what will he do to me?*

Hands moved down my back, then further, cupping my ass cheeks, fondling them lightly. My shout was a mere mumble behind the gag. I started to writhe, shaking in my bonds.

He slapped my ass hard, the noise cutting the air. The pain traveled in a burst through my flesh, down to my toes.

"Clearly, you have trouble obeying. Let's fix that."

Wondering how he meant to 'fix' me, I flooded with worry.

And also with something else.

My whole core was electric. It burned, making my breathing heavier. Wilder.

Control yourself, I demanded. *Think of a way out of this!*

But with what he had planned... nothing I did would make a difference.

He'd said he was going to break me.

And he meant it.

Current Day

I placed my hand gingerly on my mailbox, closing my eyes as if to pray. My forehead wrinkled with hard grooves, thoughts running with one simple phrase:

Acceptance letter, acceptance letter.

Bracing myself as if preparing to be punched, I tugged the panel open. As soon as I did, envelopes spilled out and across the damp ground. Groaning, I slumped my shoulders, hurrying to gather up the wet paper.

We'd been experiencing a streak of rain in the *supposedly* sunny realm of Los Angeles.

Shutting the mailbox, I slipped eagerly into the dryness of my studio apartment. The screen door hung limp on its hinges; I ignored it. The thing had been broken since I'd moved in.

Every time I call the landlord, they assure me they'll fix it soon.

Yup. Soon.

Huffing, I opened my arms and let the mail drift onto the coffee table. Dropping down in front of it, I dug through the mushy paper until I finally found what I'd been waiting for.

With trembling hands, I held the envelope before my eyes.

This is it, this has to be my acceptance into the California College of Fine Arts!

Swallowing the lump that wouldn't go away, I tore the envelope open. There, still soggy from the rain, I found my letter. Peeling it apart, I scanned the printed text rapidly. Finally, at the bottom, my answer awaited me.

Not admitted.

My heart was throttled by my sadness. *They denied me. Why?*

Scowling, I crumpled up the rejection

letter. In one great swing, it bounced off a wall, landing in the corner. With a defeated groan, I began pacing the length of the room. It wasn't a long walk, my place was painfully small.

Rejected. After everything.

What did hard work matter, if you just ended up on your last dime in a city you couldn't even afford?

Eventually I slumped onto the one other piece of furniture I owned. The mattress sat on the bare floor, covered in blankets and used quite often as a couch.

My fingers worked into my long strands of hair, absently tying it into knots.

I need a plan. Something, anything, HAS to go my way for once.

Luck had never been in my favor. I was the kid that always tripped on unseen cracks in the sidewalk, or dropped her lunch when everyone just happened to be watching.

Didn't life owe me a *little* karma?

The sharp ring of my phone cut through the air, startling me so that I yanked my hair. Flinching, I dug into the pocket of my jacket. My heart fluttered a moment as I imagined that *this* was my sign.

Had the cruel world finally called to give me a break?

The number on the screen was one I

recognized. Sighing, I clicked the button. "Hey, Mom."

"You sound so cheerful," the sarcastic voice on the other end said.

I had to crack a smile. It was true, I knew I sounded defeated. Shifting on the bed, I stretched out on my stomach and stared blankly at my coffee table. "Sorry, it's just the rain. I hate it, you know?"

It wasn't entirely a lie.

"Well, if you say so. How's everything? Have you applied to any colleges yet? Gotten into one? Sold any art?"

I wrinkled my nose. "Hah, what a barrage of questions."

My mom laughed, but I imagined her rolling her eyes. "Sweetie, it's all really the *same* question."

"I know." My attention shifted from the table, to the rest of my mail that had drifted to the floor near me. "And *you* probably know the answer already." Blinking, I noticed a single square of green among the junk-mail.

Reaching out, my fingers tugged the letter closer, balancing my cellphone between ear and shoulder.

What's this? I wondered.

I was distantly aware of my mother talking, but I'd stopped listening. There, in my hands, was the most unassuming envelope. Carefully I tore it, tugging the card free.

"Naomi," my mom snapped. "Hello? Are you there? I asked you a question."

Sitting up in a hurry, I crushed the phone in my trembling hand. "Sorry, what was the question?"

"I said, if things don't get better, you know you can always come home. If you don't get into a college soon, it'll really be your only choice. You're twenty-three, honey. I can't afford to keep you out there in LA if there's no reason for you to be there."

With a smile that was slow, yet unending once it started, I lifted the letter before my eyes. The script was soft, curled. It proclaimed exactly what I needed just then.

We'd like to extend you an offer to display your work in our gallery.

"Actually, Mom," I said softly, "Things may finally be looking up."

****

Staring at the wide glass front window, I tried to make myself stop smiling. My face was starting to hurt, but I was simply too excited.

Well, if I'm honest, the location isn't great... and I'm pretty sure the building next

10

to this is full of junkies.

I didn't care. Nothing could smother my joy.

Tugging the small wagon behind me, I pushed into the building. It was a single large room with rafters arching above. It reminded me of a warehouse, and it smelled strongly of sawdust and paint thinner.

I inhaled slowly, enjoying the scent. It reminded me of work.

Staring around, noticing the dark red walls and the lights hanging down, I didn't spot the can of brushes until I tripped over it. "Augh!" I shouted, stumbling onto my ass, the wagon of canvases tipping over.

Apparently my luck hadn't gotten better, after all.

"Are you alright?"

The voice was female, high pitched like a bird. I flinched, my cheeks burning pink. The only real damage had been to my pride. Glancing up at the speaker, I saw a woman who reminded me of a willow tree in both height *and* hair.

My laughter was forced. "I'm fine, yeah." Standing quickly, I dusted off my pants and flashed an embarrassed smile. "Sorry about that, I didn't notice the cans there."

Brown eyes, friendly and warm, looked me up and down. "It's fine, that was quite an entrance!" She extended a long arm, spindly fingers stretching. "I'm Veronica, you must be...?"

"Naomi, Naomi Starling." As I shook Veronica's hand, I noticed how cold it was.

"Oh, yes!" Laughing, she suddenly wrapped me in a hug. It was a gesture much too friendly for a first meeting.

Before I could even ask what was going on, the woman gripped my shoulders. Holding me at a distance, she studied me. "You're so *young*, I was sure you'd be ancient. Your paintings have such an old soul in them! What are you, a college kid?"

"Uh, well, 'attempted' college kid," I said with chagrin. "Haven't gotten in where I want yet—wait, you've seen my work?"

"Of course! I saw it at the craft festival on Vine last month. You weren't there, so I just grabbed one of your cards."

I flushed, recalling how I'd gotten lost and been late that day. LA traffic, combined with its one way streets, had done me in. One of the event agents had to set up *and* guard my booth for several hours.

It hit me, then, who Veronica had to be. "Wait. You're running this gallery?"

"Running is a strong word," she said, winking. Bending down to right my wagon, she started loading the canvases back inside. I crouched to help as she kept talking. "I do my best, don't get me wrong, but it's, you know." She waved her arm around her head. "This city makes running *anything* a hurdle."

"Oh," I mumbled. *I guess I shouldn't have assumed this was going to be some high-end experience. My stuff isn't well known, don't know why I thought this gallery would be my break.* Dropping the last canvas into the wagon, I straightened up.

Veronica emulated me, raising an eyebrow. Her peach lips crinkled up at one side. "I'm bad at this, that wasn't meant to make you feel depressed or anything. We run the gallery with different artists once a month, so there's plenty of time for you to make some sales. Don't worry about the money."

How could I *not* worry about the money?

I tugged at the end of my braid, once more studying the space. "Who else will be setting up their art here?"

"What do you mean?" She grabbed her hips, cocking them to the side dramatically. "Didn't you realize by now?"

Anticipation crawling up my spine.

Laughing long, loud, but without any hint of rudeness, the taller woman grabbed me by the hands and gave a squeeze. "Honey, you've got this whole space to yourself. It's yours to fill!"

"All of it?" I heard my heart more than I felt it. Everything was going numb.

Veronica's teeth sparkled in the lights. She released me so she could spread her arms, turning in place. "All of it!"

This... this is...

Dazed as I was, I wondered if I might topple over. Unsure what else to do, I looked down at my small wagon, then at the large field of blank walls.

"I think I'll need more canvases," I whispered.

- Chapter Two -
Naomi

By the end of the third day, I had managed several things.

1. Covering a single wall of the space with art I had completed before being invited to the gallery.

2. Showing Veronica that I could knock over more than just paint brushes.

3. Falling asleep in the middle of painting.

4. Actually *running out* of canvases.

Thankfully, the woman had given me a few larger pieces to work on at my heart's content; huge stretches of canvas that had been left behind from a former showing.

"Do what you want with them." Veronica had shrugged, sipping what was certainly her fifth cup of coffee. I think it was all she ever drank.

Blown away by the opportunity, I'd propped the large squares on the wall, set up my paints, and begun experimenting. The gallery was starting to look like an actual... well, gallery.

With my art filling the room, I still

wanted to finish one of the bigger pieces. It would be perfect for the section that could be seen from the front window.

Dipping my brush, I let the colors guide me, becoming so wrapped up in watching the art come to life. Covered in sweat, splashes of paint, and smelling like turpentine, I was a true mess.

But I didn't care.

This was what I loved, and I embraced it. It was why I wanted to attend an art college in the first place. Growing up, no one in my small town had cared about art. I was mocked by everyone, and I always felt out of place.

Then, one day, I'd found a pamphlet for California College of Fine Arts. Seeing the photos of people—working away proudly—I'd felt an instant kinship.

My decision was obvious.

However, I'd gotten a late start on applying. Gathering the money needed to make a portfolio, and ultimately, to fly out to LA, had been hard work. That was why the past three years of rejection letters was soul-crushing.

But I was willing to scrape by on what tiny money I could manage. I was even willing to endure the snide remarks my family made each time my mother sent me some financial help.

If it got me closer to my dreams, I'd do

anything.

Staring at the mixture of black as it bled into green, I didn't hear the door open behind me. I certainly wasn't aware of the crisp, perfectly shined shoes as they crossed the room.

If he hadn't spoken, I might have painted for another hour, unaware I had a visitor at all.

His voice was smooth, rolling like cream and syrup mixed together. "You move beautifully, like a ballerina."

I jumped, kicking over my color pallet. It splattered to the floor, and his compliment about me moving like a ballerina became a cruel lie. Twisting around, I brushed my hair away, staring at the man who was talking, apparently, to me.

His outfit was darker than the paint on my canvas, a crisp vest over dove-grey sleeves. With skin paler than mine, hair ebony in even the bright lights, this stranger was a perfect combination of colorless tones.

Then I noticed his eyes, and my opinion changed.

They were intense, thoughtful, and bluer than they had any right to be.

Who *was* this man?

"Uh," I said, feeling very out of my element.

"Forgive me, I saw you working through the window." He indicated with his sharp jaw, a smile cutting across his face. "I didn't know there was an art gallery here."

"We're not open till tomorrow," I said, my voice distant. Shaking my head, clearing the haze and my throat all at once, I refocused on the stranger. *Did he say I moved beautifully?*

He frowned, strolling to the side to get a better look at my work in progress. "I see. Will this be ready by tomorrow, do you suppose?"

Blinking, I shifted around to follow him, finally turning to face my own canvas. Peering at it, I wondered what had made him so interested.

It was more abstract than my usual stuff, and while I was enjoying creating it, I didn't think it looked particularly special. "I'm going to try to complete it, yes, why do you ask?"

"Well, I'd like to buy it, of course."

"What? But it's not done and... and you don't even know how much I'm going to charge for it!" This had never happened to me before, my mind was swimming in dark water.

"It doesn't matter."

The way he looked me up and down made me shiver. It wasn't a cold sensation, though. Oddly, the ball twisting inside of me was rather... warm.

Get it together!

There was something about this man that was setting me on edge. It had to be more than just his shockingly good looks.

"Whatever you charge," he said, "I'll pay it."

Lost, I heard myself speak before I could control it. "*Why?*"

Wrinkling his forehead, the man linked his hands behind his back and eyed me like I'd made a joke. "Why? Because I like it, but more than that, I enjoyed the glimpse I had of watching *you* create it."

Blushing furiously, I stared around the room. I was trying to avoid gawking at him without being so obvious. "Uh, haha, I see. Well, I'm afraid I can't help you right now. Like I said, we're not open until tomorrow, so if you want to come back then..."

"You won't let me watch you paint?"

I jerked around to meet his even stare. My mouth opened, but no sound escaped. It was such a strange question.

His eyes were serious. I knew he wasn't joking.

"Who *are* you?" I asked.

His smile went sideways, like I'd said something funny. "You're not from around here, I take it." Before I could respond, my neck heating in a moment of insulted anger, he lifted a palm. "I'm Seth Hart, and you are?"

"Naomi Starling," I said warily.

"Starling," he mused. "I like that. Well, Ms. Starling, let me just clarify this. You don't want me here, because you are not open yet. However, you'll be done with your work tomorrow, when I *am* allowed to come by and purchase your art?"

"...Yes."

He ran his fingers through his short hair. "Perhaps I can make that work. Have a good evening, Ms. Starling." For a moment, I thought he might bow. I was relieved when he only turned on a polished heel, exiting out the door.

Staring after him, I rubbed at my dirty cheek in wonderment.

Who the hell was that? Was I supposed to know him, like he implied?

I'd encountered some 'characters' in Los Angeles during my time, eccentric people didn't surprise me. But there was something especially odd about such a handsome, well dressed man complimenting me out of the blue.

And on top of that, offering to buy my art without asking the price?

Maybe he was super rich, I mused. Cracking my back, I sighed deeply, surveying my canvas. *Will he really come back and buy it?*

Smiling at the idea, I reached down and grabbed a paper tag. Taping it to the wall, I scribbled with a pen in my messy way, marking the unfinished canvas. It read: five thousand dollars.

It was childish to mark it so high, but it was a small bit of revenge for putting me on the spot like he had. It was crazy to think the piece would sell for that much, I wasn't stupid; I had plenty of other art to sell. I wasn't shooting myself in the foot, not really.

Leaning back, I eyed my work in progress. *Worst case, he doesn't buy it, no one buys it, and I drop the price the next day to something realistic.*

Still...

What if he really *did* buy it?

"No," I told myself, laughing. "Impossible."

Grabbing the paintbrush, I went back to work.

****

The morning of the gallery opening came suddenly.

To me, anyway.

Groggy after a late night of painting, I stumbled through my shower and cup of coffee before the reality finally hit me.

Tonight is my show. My show, mine!

Holy hell.

Dressing in the nicest gown I had—a long thing of perfectly smooth black that dipped low and showed off my shoulders and more—I did my makeup as best as I could with my shaking hands.

I was ready in a flash, spending the next few hours fidgeting around my apartment.

Finally, with a deep inhale of air, I gathered my purse and hurried to the gallery space.

The evening was warm, though I couldn't tell how much of that was from my nervous sweating. As I approached the gallery, I saw that the large front window was... different.

Within a few feet, I was able to tell what had changed.

There, in scrolling, curly letters, someone had painted the words, 'Gallery of Wings' and then below, 'the Art of Naomi Starling.'

Seeing this, my grin spread wide. Through the glass, the place was lit up like an orange sky, the red walls adding to the effect.

Pushing my way in, I saw Veronica bent over a table. The tall woman was busily setting up stacks of cards. She turned at the sound of me entering, and we flashed each other excited looks.

"Do you like it?" Veronica gushed, her hands clasping together.

I didn't need to ask *what* she was referring to, I just stepped forward and wrapped the woman in a tight hug. "Veronica, this is amazing! Did you set this all up by yourself?"

"Psh." She laughed, disengaging so she could finish adjusting things on the table. "It was nothing! You did all the real work, the art looks fantastic."

"Do you think I'll sell anything?" I didn't want to ask so bluntly, to reveal my fears, but in the moment it had simply slipped out. Biting my lip, I studied the woman's face for any hint of judgment. I only found her crooked smile.

"Naomi, honestly. You're worrying too much. I'm sure you'll sell *something* on your first night. Now, help me with these registration cards. We need them so people can bid on the art."

Hunkering down, I helped her finish setting up.

We were just in time.

As the evening turned the outside sky

into a navy bruise, the warmth of the gallery seemed to draw people in. They lined up, and they didn't stop. Quickly, the place was full.

People strolled around, drinking wine and chattering about what they saw. I was too nervous to listen in, so I hovered by a corner. Someone—maybe Veronica—must have told someone I was the artist on display, though.

Before long, I was smothered in a wave of questions from pure strangers.

"How long did this take you?"

"Have you painted for a long time?"

"What school do you go to?"

"Do you plan to have another showing in the future?"

"What was your inspiration?"

By the end of the first hour, I was dizzy. I swam through the crowd, looking for Veronica. The tall woman was caught in her own sea of people, juggling paper sheets and answering questions.

Ducking my head, I wormed towards a far wall, trying to become invisible. Glancing around, I noticed the little cards on some of my canvases had been filled out with bids. My heart throbbed with the excitement of knowing people were buying my work.

My brain tingled, the memory of the night before tugging at me.

I wonder if that guy, Seth, will come by and purchase the big piece he liked.

I was tempted to go look, to see if it had any bids. Oddly, the sheer chance that it didn't kept me from looking.

The chance that he hadn't...

Stop, don't be weird. You don't even know the guy. Rubbing my neck, feeling the dampness from the heat of such a crammed space, I sighed. This was no time to ponder if I'd see that handsome stranger again. Already, people were swarming me once more, demanding my attention, making me feel claustrophobic.

And then, just like that, it was all over.

Waving farewell to the last stragglers leaving the gallery, I marveled that I had made it through in one piece. "Bye! Have a good night!" I called out. Locking the door, I promptly sat on the floor. "Oh my goodness. That was insane."

"Right?" Veronica laughed, flopping across the long table. Her eyes twinkled on me. "But it was fun, wasn't it? How did you like it, be honest."

I covered my eyes with an arm as the lights above blinded me. "It was amazing." Sitting up, I gripped the edge of the table. My nose was close to Veronica's, the willowy woman smirking at the clear anticipation on my face. "Please tell me I sold some stuff."

"Actually," Veronica started, her expression twitching. It was strange, seeing such delight morph to concern. "There was *one* person who was a buyer tonight."

"Oh." My belly clenched with dread. "Just one?"

After everything, to sell so little...

Veronica frowned, her fingers gliding over a stack of papers. "I don't know how to say this. Um, you might have an obsessed fan, or something."

Knotting my brow, I settled onto my knees. "Me, a fan? Besides *you?*"

"I like your work, don't get me wrong, but this is... different. Here, just look." With an expression that bordered on dubiousness, Veronica slid a piece of paper across the table.

Grabbing it, I lifted it close and read the form. "I don't understand. This is just a sheet listing all of my artwork."

"No, Naomi. It's a list of all your work that *sold* tonight."

We stared at each other, the clarity sinking in like a heavy stone. "You're telling me one person bought everything? One person, they bought it *all?*"

Veronica didn't give an answer, but she didn't need to. This was strange, we both knew it, and it marred what should have been amazing news.

Tentatively, I rolled my eyes down that paper, terrified to read the signature at the bottom. But I had to know, I needed to see the name of the person who would have the money, the desire, to purchase my entire collection.

The name was scrawled beautifully, the practiced penmanship of someone who knew their signature would be read over and over.

It was a name that made my skin prickle.

Seth Hart.

- Chapter Three -
Naomi

I stared into my glass of wine, sitting on the floor of the gallery with a bottle between me and Veronica. She had insisted we celebrate, and I had little in the way of resistance. Veronica didn't seem to care that I was exhausted, she just poured me another drink, stating I deserved it.

Watching me closely, she asked the question that had been burning between us. "You *really* don't know who he is, Naomi?"

"You're saying that like I should. No, I don't have a clue. Why?"

"Well." She tilted her head back, that mop of hair waving like there was a breeze in the room. "Here's the thing. I actually do recognize his name."

"What?" I almost spilled my wine as I leaned forward. "Why didn't you say anything before?"

Shrugging, Veronica drained the last of her glass and pursed her lips. "I assumed you knew. Most folks around here do. Listen, it's sort of like... You know, you assume people know some names by default."

Unless she was talking about Santa

Clause, then no, I didn't know many names by 'default.' "Spill it. Who is he?"

Pouring out the last of the bottle, Veronica tapped the rim of her drink in thought. "He's majorly rich, but that's not how I know of him. Seth Hart is one of the biggest financial contributors to CCFA, and I work with a lot of people from there in this industry."

"CCFA." My heart skipped. "The California College of Fine Arts!?"

"Yeah, that's right. Why do you look so pale?"

Touching my cheek, I tried to slow down my brain. My thoughts were buzzing. "That's— that's the college I've been trying to get into."

Veronica gaped at me. "I'm trying to be relaxed here, for your sake. But that's an insane coincidence, Naomi. Like, extremely insane."

Hanging my head, I breathed out loudly. The scent of the alcohol was bothering me, making my stomach ripple with sourness. "I know it is."

Is this just a coincidence? Fate?

What does it mean?

"No," Veronica said. "You don't. Here, this is the part I was waiting to give up." Digging into her pocket, she pulled out a crinkled card, offering it like it might bite. I reached for it just as reluctantly.

Turning it over, I realized it was a business card.

"Why did he give you this?" I asked.

"He wanted me to tell you to call him, he... he wanted to know if you took commissions." Veronica hesitated, biting her lip. "I said I wasn't sure. He insisted I give you that, so you could reach him."

I had a strong urge to throw the card away, but part of me was intrigued. "How long did you guys talk for?"

"Not long. I was busy, and he pretty much just handed me the bidding form and a blank check." She laughed, shaking her head in disbelief. "You understand how much money you made tonight, right?" Veronica searched my dazed eyes, her tone softer. "You don't need to take his personal commission for more cash, is my point."

I was still staring at the card. "Money aside, this guy might be my in. He'd be able to help me get past admissions at the college, if he has as much pull as it sounds."

What would he want from me, though, in exchange?

Is this really about my art?

Veronica grabbed the empty bottle, standing with a groan as she cracked her back. "Well, this gallery is going to be done, now. Your stuff will stay up for the month, but you don't need to come here, since it's all sold. I can cut you your share, and then." The wine bottle crashed loudly into the trash. "Then, I guess you can do whatever you like."

Tucking the business card into my pocket, I stood as well, lost in my own head.

"Naomi."

"Yeah?" I looked up to find the worried face of my new friend. *How fast, but yes, we did become friends.*

"Just remember, you don't need to call him. You don't *need* to do anything, alright?"

Can I really just do nothing? I wondered.

Frowning, I took one more look around the room, finally ending on the large piece, the one Seth had walked in on me painting last night.

My mind was a blur, considering all my options. There was potential in this venture for the one thing I really wanted.

It's another chance. How many of those did life give us?

With a forced smile, I faced Veronica, holding out a hand. "Thank you, I'll keep in touch."

When we shook, I noticed how hard Veronica was gripping me. Suddenly, it turned into a fierce hug, leaving us both breathless.

"Don't do anything dumb," Veronica mumbled into my ear.

I wish I could have told her I wouldn't.

In the end, I said nothing.

****

For the third time, I lifted my cell phone, finger hovering over the buttons. Seth's card lay on the bed beside me, but I didn't need to look at it. By now, I'd managed to unintentionally ingrain his phone number into my mind.

Sighing, I lowered my cellphone, staring at the screen. It displayed the time, reminding me it was after ten at night. It gave me an easy out. *He's probably asleep. Also, who makes a business call this late?*

My whole body and brain were vibrating; anxious, unable to relax. Veronica's warning, as if I could call it anything else, rumbled in my subconscious.

She's wrong, I DO need to do this. It's such an opportunity to get an upper hand, to get into that school.

Plus... I'd get to see Seth again.

That man had left an impression on me, even if I didn't want to admit it. He was crisp on the edges, a coolness with something far more wild beneath the surface of his cocky smirk.

The slow burn of intrigue in my belly had me clenching my thighs.

Once more, I lifted the phone.

The worse that happens, is he doesn't answer, and I leave a message.

I debated if maybe, just maybe, the worse that could happen was actually making the phone call at all.

No, he didn't seem dangerous. He bought all of my art, I have enough money now to stay out here for some time.

Is it crazy to want to find out how much he'd offer for a commission, and if he'd agree to assist me into CCFA?

Biting my lower lip, I typed out his number. Pressing the phone to my ear, I listened to the metallic ringing, preparing myself for what I would say to the machine.

On the second ring, the line 'clicked' and someone began speaking.

"Seth Hart, who's calling, please?"

The voice wasn't the familiar, rich baritone of the man I'd met so briefly. This was someone else, calm and almost flat—and not an answering machine. Confused, I cleared my throat. "Uh, hello, I'm looking for Seth."

"Of course, but may I ask who's calling?"

33

Had I imagined the tart edge to that reply? "Sorry, this is Naomi Starling, he left me a message to—"

"Oh!" The person suddenly became very pleasant. "Yes, of course, one moment, I'll transfer you to his main line."

A spark of indignation flared. With the effort Seth had made, buying everything and leaving his card, I thought he *had* given me his main phone number.

Veronica said he was pretty important. I guess he doesn't really know me, so filtering calls makes sense.

Was it fair of me to be insulted?

The line was silent, to the point that I wondered if I had been disconnected. *Seriously? Did I just get the cold shoulder?* Perhaps Seth wasn't as interested in my art as he had seemed. Had Veronica misunderstood?

I was too tired to deal with being given the runaround. My hand moved, ready to end the call.

"Hello, Ms. Starling?" When he spoke, it created a familiar thrill down my spine.

That's him! Seth was on the line.

"Yes," I said, tugging my hair nervously. "I mean, yes, it's me."

"So you got my message."

"Ah, yeah, Veronica gave it to me after

34

the show."

"It was a lovely gallery, your work was beautiful." He made a sound, I couldn't tell if it was him breathing out or chuckling. "But, on topic, she told you about my offer?"

I shifted the phone to my other ear, reaching out to pick up his business card. Even with the crinkles in it from Veronica's pocket, the printed ink was sharp, immaculate. "She sort of did. According to her, you want a commission, but..."

"But?"

"But, you... did you really buy all of my art, for just yourself?" The words rushed free in a whirl as the shock finally caught up to me. "All of it? I have the check from Veronica. If this isn't a joke, I just... why do you want, or need, any more from me?"

There was a heavy silence. I opened my mouth, ready to apologize for my abrupt questions. Seth halted me with a low, throaty laugh that couldn't be confused for anything else. "Ms. Starling, slow down. Yes, I bought everything you had. Is it so wrong if I would enjoy *more* from you?"

His emphasis on the word 'more' made my tongue very dry. I realized I'd started crushing the business card in my hand. Dropping it, I wiped my palm on my leg, wondering what to say. *What does he really want from me, why does he like my work so much?*

"Ms. Starling," he said.

"Y—yes?"

"I can tell you're a little nervous. Please, just hear me out. I'm only offering you some work, after all, nothing more."

"Nothing more?" I asked warily.

"What else could I offer?" I swore I could hear him smirk over the phone.

Swallowing, I began again. "There is something else you could offer me."

His silence was uncomfortable, it turned my arm hairs into sharp prickles. Seconds later, he whispered, "What would you like from me, Ms. Starling?"

Dammit. Why was his voice so sexy?

I pushed my uncertainty away. I needed to push forward while I had the opportunity. "There's a college I'm trying to get into. You're apparently pretty important to them. I was hoping... maybe... that you could help get accepted."

His sigh was languid, steamy. "I see. So you don't care about the money, so much as the prestige."

I had no answer to that.

"Let's go with that desire of yours, then. You want something, something it seems only I can give you... and I would love to have a personal art piece created by your hands."

Flooding with elation, I started nodding, even though he couldn't see it. "Oh, yes, that—"

"But," he cut me off, "There is a slight twist."

Oh god, what could that be? With my heart throbbing, I mumbled the shakiest words ever. "What twist is that?"

"I don't want you to paint on canvas. I actually have a wall in my home I would like you to use it for your base."

Crinkling the bridge of my nose, I parsed this information carefully. "You want me to paint inside your house?"

"Exactly. I have a section that is utterly too bland, I think your work would look amazing there."

"I'd obviously have to come to your place to do this." Swallowing, my pulse racing, I pressed on with my real question. "When I finish, you'd agree to help me?"

"Yes. I'll happily write a letter of recommendation to the CCFA dean for you, once the job is complete." Seth hummed briefly. "I'll also buy you the materials for this mural, pay for your meals while you're here, send transportation, and anything else you might need during your visits. Does that sound fair?"

I dropped the phone, the device clanking from my bed to the floor. That was more than I imagined. He would get me into the college without a doubt.

A personal letter!

I heard a noise, and looking down, noticed my phone blinking. The distant sound was clearly Seth. Scrambling, I picked it up and heard the tail end of his sentence. "—alright, Ms. Starling?"

"Sorry, sorry, I uh, what was that last thing?"

"I asked if everything sounded alright? If so, I can send someone to pick you up tomorrow, and we can go over the contract."

Looking around my small apartment, I noticed the crumpled rejection letter in the corner. I hadn't touched it since I'd thrown it away so angrily.

This is it, this is the break I've needed so badly.

"Yes," I said with a stunned smile. "Yes, that sounds just perfect."

****

I'd been too excited to sleep well.

When the sun started rising, I gave up

and rolled out of bed, landing gently on the hard floor. I ended up wandering around my small apartment, debating what to bring, how to dress, and even what shoes to wear.

He said he'd provide the supplies, I guess I don't need to bring much.

Tugging on a pair of tight jeans, as well as a comfortable purple top that walked the line between casual and fancy, I stood by the window. Seth had told me, before I had hung up, that he'd send a car over around nine in the morning.

Glancing at the clock on my stove, I shifted uneasily and leaned on the wall. *Any minute now, but how will I know what car is for me?*

As if on cue, a vehicle that was far too fancy for the area rolled slowly around the corner. It was black, reminding me of a killer whale on the hunt. I didn't know much about cars, but I was wise enough to understand that this thing, whatever it was, had to cost a fortune.

Oh my god, it might as well be a limo.

When the driver stepped out, I noted his expensive outfit matched the car perfectly. He turned his shiny sunglasses up towards my window. I ducked out of sight, wincing.

This was too much. I was out of my element, and I hadn't even gotten *in* the car yet.

My phone buzzed, a text from a number I didn't recognize. It read, 'Your car has arrived, please go outside, Ms. Starling.'

So, I mused, *Seth gave my number to his driver.*

Hiding was impossible.

It was also pointless.

Frowning, I tucked my cell into my purse. Wandering down the steps, I caught one of my neighbors staring at me from their window. Blushing wildly, I quickened my pace.

Wonderful, I'll be the talk of the town.

Stepping into the early sunlight, I shielded myself from the blinding glint of the car. The driver waved, opening the back door as I approached. "Ms. Starling, after you," the well dressed man said.

I recognized his voice; he had answered the phone last night when I first tried to call Seth.

"Thanks," I mumbled, slipping inside. Settling on the expensive seat, I tested the plush material. *This is nicer than my whole apartment.*

The driver shut his door, adjusting his mirror. Watching him, I said, "So you work for Seth, I assume?" *What a ridiculous question.*

"Indeed." He nodded, turning the wheel and inching the vehicle silently down the street.

It was smooth, a well oiled machine in every sense. "I'm Mr. Hart's personal chauffeur, he usually sends me for his important clients."

So I'm an important client, am I?

Turning slightly, I watched the city move past the window, taking note of where we were going. It was obvious we were heading out of the dregs of LA and into the upper areas of Hollywood. *I guess I shouldn't be too surprised that he'd have a house up here.*

The colors turned from brown and gold, to fresh green and white. The road was winding, curling along so I had a lovely view of the city below. It was a landscape I didn't get to enjoy much. I found myself wide-eyed, a child in glee. *It's easy to forget how beautiful this city is when you're down on your luck.*

It wasn't a long drive, the car turned around a sharp bend then slowed before a pair of wrought iron gates. I almost laughed at the sheer cliché nature of it all. We rolled through the barrier as it parted, the path turning into paved brick.

Then the house finally came into view.

That's no house, that's a mansion!

I covered my mouth, baffled by the immense size of the place. The land was surrounded by lemon and fig trees, hiding the home from the outside world. It was a picturesque realm of privacy, vibrant and so

41

unlike the area I lived in.

The house sprawled with shingled roofs, tall tower like spires; old school in style and in complete contrast of the squat homes in LA. I'd figured Seth was well off, but this was simply outlandish.

"Here we are," the driver said casually, pulling around the side and parking on a flat circle of stone. There were other cars there. Of course he would own multiple vehicles. All of them were shining bright, a rainbow of colors.

But I was still just gawking up at the mansion.

"Seth lives *here?*"

"Of course," the driver chuckled.

Shaking my head, I sat there until the older man exited, coming around to open my door. He offered a hand, but I didn't take it. Sliding out into the air, I craned my neck to try and see the whole house at once. "This is amazing," I stated.

The driver flashed a slight smile, closing my door and gesturing. "Follow me, please, Ms. Starling."

Both him and Seth, calling me that, it makes me sound so important. I'm too young to be a Ms. Anything.

We entered through the tall front door, the wood pure white, the handle bronze and sparkling. Inside, I inhaled in a great rush, staring around at the view.

The entrance room was huge, a wide circle that extended upwards. From the plush carpet under me, to the sparkling chandeliers above, the whole place was opulent. A curling staircase stretched from my left, going up and around a long hallway above.

There were massive bookshelves, curved bay windows, and plush couches arranged with intent. In the walls there were several wide openings, clearly leading to other rooms.

As I let my gaze roam, I realized only one door was closed.

It was set into the side of the giant staircase, bright gold, like it was coated in lacquer. It was out of place among all the pearl and ivory.

I had so many questions; I was too overwhelmed to voice them.

"Ms. Starling," a familiar voice called, causing me to look at the railing above. Seth was watching, leaning against the curling wood that kept him from falling to his death. He was dressed as sharp as the first time, dark charcoal and a pressed jacket.

In one hand, I saw he had a small glass, but I couldn't tell what he was drinking. "I'm glad you made it, how was the drive?"

"Good," I said too quietly. "Uh, good! It was very scenic."

He nodded, waltzing down the stairs in lazy, confident strides. Swirling his glass, he took another sip, then gestured to the driver with it. "Thank you, Corbin, you can go. I might need you later, if Ms. Starling desires to return home."

If I desire? I was puzzled by the way he had worded that.

Corbin, as he was apparently called, bowed his head to the both of us. In a second, he'd exited out the front door. As it closed sharply, it finally hit me.

I'm alone with Seth Hart.

He paused at the bottom of the stairs, seeming to consider me with those sapphire eyes of his. "Welcome, officially, to my home."

Watching his elegant fingers, how they drummed on the hard railing, I laughed uneasily. "Thanks, it's quite... I mean, I don't even know how to put this. It's amazing, really."

"Thank you." He inclined his head, then reached out to offer me his hand. "Let me show you around."

I reached out and took his smooth palm, hoping he didn't notice how sweaty mine was.

Together, we wandered up into the hall above. There was a length of white wall on one side, railing on the other. The view below was beautiful; I could see the luxuriously designed carpet, and once more, that alluring golden door.

Where does it go? Is it a fancy closet?

Seth led me along the corridor, pointing out studies, foyers, and a grand marble bathroom. I noticed a number of bedrooms, but none that looked particularly lived in.

The tour continued downstairs, where he showed me his grand kitchen. It was modern in its touches, despite the mansion's vintage feel.

A pair of huge, sliding glass doors displayed the backyard. It was packed with shady green grass and purple flowers. Most notable was the crisply-clear pool shaped like a kidney bean.

There was obviously much more to see, but Seth walked me back to the kitchen, ending the tour. Grabbing a bottle from a cabinet, he poured me a drink of something red. "Do you like it?" he asked, handing me the crystal glass, a thing that I was nervous to hold.

Frowning, I squinted into the cup. *How expensive is this glass, or this wine?* Sipping the liquid, I watched him over the rim in thought. "It's very impressive, but it's also so big! Do you live here all alone?"

"For the most part. I have Corbin, and often clients or guests will come by." Shrugging, he set his empty glass by the sink. "I

45

entertain a lot, as well. Hence, why I wanted your services."

"Right." I blinked, trying to imagine how fancy a gathering here had to be. *How does he afford all of this? What does he do to make money?* "Can you show me where I'm supposed to paint? I didn't see anywhere obvious in the rooms you showed me." Lifting an eyebrow, a thought hit me. I pointed out of the kitchen towards the main entrance room. "It is out there?"

"Precisely." He flashed those perfect pearly teeth.

I returned the smile, almost relieved. "I thought so, that gold door was the only place you didn't show me. So is that another dining room down there, or—"

"No," he snapped, startling me. For the first time since I'd met him, Seth's lovely features were twisted in a harsh frown. "No, not there." His blue eyes softened, as if he had realized how curt his tone was. "Sorry, that room is off limits."

I'd frozen under his explosion. Remembering to breathe, I inhaled slowly. "Oh, I didn't know."

"Of course, how could you have?" Gesturing towards the archway, he guided me back out to the main room.

I shot one look at that golden door,

wondering why his reaction had been so visceral. "If I'm not painting in there, then where did you mean?"

Didn't he say it was out here?

Seth chuckled, I followed his eyes as he rolled them up to the long length of white wall above. It was where he had been standing when I'd entered, leaning on that intricate railing.

"I'm painting that?" I gasped, nearly dropping my wine glass. "That whole thing?"

"That is exactly what I am hoping for, Ms. Starling."

Looking at it again, taking in the size, the knowledge that it would be the first thing people would see when they entered the mansion hit me.

I felt a flush of both pride, and fear.

Lifting my glass, I drained the contents, then exhaled loudly. "That's going to take me at least two weeks, Seth."

"I know, that's why I said I'd take care of anything you'd need."

"Yeah, you mentioned buying me supplies."

Seth tilted his head, reaching out to gently take my empty glass. "No, Ms. Starling. I mean *anything*."

The base of my neck warmed at his words. "I don't understand, what else could I need besides paints?"

Tapping a finger around the rim of the glass, Seth narrowed his cobalt eyes and laughed. "For starters, food. On top of that, as I said, I'm willing to let Corbin escort you back and forth. However..." He trailed off, his gaze moving back up to the hall. "There's a few spare rooms here. I'm more than happy to allow you to stay until this mural is complete."

"Stay here?" The idea was exciting. I'd never been in a mansion, staying here would be like a vacation. I'd have access to a pool, privacy, and I was sure the food would be amazing, if the wine was any hint.

I also felt the rumble of my nerves.

Everything here is so expensive, what if I break something?

And could I handle sleeping here, knowing an intimidating, far-too-sexy-guy like Seth Hart was nearby? Just imagining him under the same roof was a bit much.

"I... I'm not sure if I'll stay," I mumbled.

"It's fine," he said, lifting a hand to calm me. It didn't help, my heart still raced. "For now, let's just get the paperwork signed. You're free to come and go. I'll outline in the contract what areas of my home you can peruse at your leisure."

The way he implied that I wasn't allowed in every room made me shoot a curious glance

48

at that gold door over his shoulder.

"Shall we, then?" His sharp cheek bones stood out when he smiled.

"Sure," I said, trying to focus on him. "Let's do this."

Once more he gave me his hand, and once more, I took it.

This time, I knew it would be impossible not to notice how clammy my skin was.

Or how I was trembling.

- Chapter Four -
Naomi

The contract ended up being far more in depth than I expected.

A stack of papers, thick as my wrist, outlined everything from liability, to timeline, to rules of the house. Flipping through it, I gave it a once over before simply staring at Seth. "Is this really necessary?"

"I have a very private life, Ms. Starling. I need you to understand what you can, and cannot, do while you are here." He folded his hands together, watching me over them as he sat behind his grand desk.

We had relocated to his study for the contract signing, a room entirely too dark for my taste. On the walls, I saw placards and awards. I also couldn't help but notice a few bare sections. Recently bare, I felt, and wondered if some of my art from the gallery was meant to hang there.

"That's fine and all, Seth, but this is just so much! Is there a break down, a summary? Just tell me the basics that would keep me from getting the letter of admission I need." I heard my own frustration.

Had my false professional aura already

cracked?

"I need you to read it all. But, if you want the basics, fine." He lifted a hand, ticking off on his fingers as he spoke. "You can come and go as you please, but you're not allowed to bring anyone here without my permission. Eat any of the food in the fridge, but do not order takeout. If you need anything else, just tell Corbin, he can get it for you. Don't go in my bedroom, it's the master room on the first floor. Don't take any photos, none of that social networking is tolerated here."

The idea of him getting angry because his mansion ended up on Pinterest almost broke my composure. Lifting an eyebrow, I fought to keep the sarcasm from my voice. "Is that *all?*"

"No," he returned my tone, "But you know the rest."

"I can go in the yard?" I asked. When he nodded, I went on. "And the bedrooms along this corridor where I'm painting?" Again, he nodded. "Alright. So it's just that gold door that you want me to stay away from."

Seth's eyes melted from blue to black. "Forget it even exists, Ms. Starling. No matter what you see."

No matter what I see? Was he trying to make me mad with curiosity?

"Could you give me some leeway? I just

want to know where it goes, why can't I know?"

"Because it's a rule," he said slowly, deliberately. His eyes met mine, hard as marble. It was a struggle not to buckle under his intensity. "Can you follow rules, Ms. Starling?"

"Of course." I sighed, trying to ease the mood with a gentle smile. "You can call me Naomi, you know."

"I prefer Ms. Starling. Now, please, sign." He slid the contract closer to me.

The restrictions weren't terrible, they just felt a little out of place. Why was he being so secretive? *I mean,* I thought to myself, *No takeout?* Was the pizza guy going to spill the beans about Seth's home? Who would care?

I ran my eyes over the page that explained what I would be given; food, a lavish bedroom, the letter of recommendation. He had also, strangely, given me access to a wardrobe of clothing.

Why he had a collection of women's clothing, I had no clue.

It seems like an amazing deal. Why do I get this strange feeling there's something insidious going on here?

If I was going to back down, this was the moment. Standing, leaving, maybe watching Seth's confidence crack as I told him I was no longer interested... all of that rippled through my mind.

Everything came back to the college.

I'd struggled for years, gone through so much.

It's the only chance I have.

I wasn't disillusioned enough to think three rejection letters wasn't a pattern.

Crushing the pen, I scrawled my name and slid everything back to him. A new, thicker knot grew in my belly as I officially agreed to the situation.

"Well done," he said, signing as well. "I'll get you a copy later. For now, let me show you what you have to work with."

Seth brought me to a closet in the hallway, revealing the contents. It was full of every sort of paint brush, every color I could ever need. The supplies were high quality, I knew it all cost a fortune.

It was a painter's dream, and my grin crossed ear to ear.

"But," I asked, walking to the long stretch of white wall, brushing my fingers over it lightly. "What do you want me to paint?"

"Whatever you'd like." He shrugged. "I've loved everything you've painted that I've seen, I trust you to make the right choice. It's *you* that I want." His smirk turned my throat into a barren wasteland.

Then, I noticed how close he was. The hall was tight, the railing inclining people to naturally stand near the wall. Seth stood over me, his face sharp as a knife in the deep shadows.

In my ears, my heart was deafening, smothering my voice. "What do you mean, you want me?"

"Your skill," he whispered, eyes rich and heated. "What you can do, how you do it, that's what I'm after. Nothing you create could be wrong, because *you* made it, Ms. Starling."

Could he hear my rapid breathing, or smell my fear?

What is this, what does he mean?

Seth leaned back, erasing the magnetic pressure in a snap. He was closed off all over again. "Now, I have some things to take care of. If you need anything, just come find me. Barring that, call Corbin, you should have his number from when he texted you this morning."

On perfectly shined shoes, Seth turned, silently trudging down the stairs. I watched him go, only starting to control my pulse when I was sure he was out of earshot.

Slumping against the cool wall, one hand clutched the front of my shirt. My laugh was weak and strained. Seth had cornered me without me seeing it happen. He'd hovered

54

over me, stealing my awareness until I had focused on nothing but him.

I'd known he was intense, but this...
What have I gotten myself into?

****

It was evening before I decided to take a break.

I'd spent most of my time plotting out the general layout for the painting, then it was down to the slow process of prepping the wall. The section was long, it took me several steps to go from one end to the next.

The left part ended at the staircase, the right connected with an archway that opened into other rooms, including my closet of paints, and the guest area I'd been offered.

Wiping my forehead, I tested my sore muscles. I craved a shower, was I was allowed to use the facilities here? *Seth has the contract, I don't have a copy still, hmn.*

Frowning, I decided it would be safer to find him and ask, instead of risking upsetting him.

Wandering down the stairs, I passed by the gold door. Absently, I slowed down to stare at it. I surveyed the entrance room. *There's no one here, is there? Would he know if I peeked?*

55

I chewed the inside of my cheek. The temptation was pulling at me, made worse by the demand that I *not* go inside. I wasn't the kind of person who broke the rules.

I had the power to resist temptation.

Think of the letter.

Finally, I slumped my shoulders and forced myself to walk into the kitchen. *I'm not ready to risk losing my chance at CCAD for something so dumb.*

Unsure where to find anything, I peered into the fridge, looking for water. I spotted a tray of glistening, chocolate covered strawberries. They made my stomach tight, reminding me I hadn't had lunch or dinner.

Ugh, can I eat those? I can't recall any of the rules, where is Seth?

Wanting to make an effort, I prowled the house. It was a futile search, I discovered nothing but more rooms and more books. After strolling blankly down some halls, I returned to the kitchen and peered out the large glass doors.

The yard was dim, night starting to creep in. The lights in the trees, sparkling on silvery strings, gave everything a pretty glow. The pool, especially, was beautiful. It muted my hunger, reminding me instead about my sweat and filth.

Pulling out my cellphone, I dialed

Corbin.

"Hello?" His voice was polite, precise.

"Hey, this is Naomi. Listen, I can't find Seth and I have a question. Is it alright if I use the pool here?"

"Of course, Mr. Hart instructed me to inform you, in this potential scenario, that there are bathing suites in the closet in the first guest room upstairs. Anything else?"

"Yes." I turned, eyeballing over my shoulder. "Are these strawberries up for grabs?"

****

Sometime later, I was soaking in the delightfully warm water of the pool.

The air was fragrant, I could hear insects chirping. My elbows were propped up on the smooth stone around the edge; my lower body, clad in a teal bikini from the closet, was submerged.

The sensation of the crystal water was melting my knotted muscles. I'd had a pool when I was younger, but it had been years since I'd gotten to indulge like this.

Gleefully, I reached into the mostly empty tray, plucking up another strawberry. They had been dipped in various chocolates; I'd eaten the dark ones, first.

Chewing thoughtfully, I kicked my feet and sighed. *Alright, this is pretty nice.*

"Enjoying yourself?"

I painfully swallowed the chunk of food I had come close to choking on.

There, standing in the open doorway of the kitchen, was Seth.

He wore a tight tank-top that did nothing to hide the row of abdominals cascading down to his lower stomach. His long, navy shorts exposed his crafted calves where he leaned.

After only seeing him in fancy outfits, I couldn't help but stare.

The fact I could see his arms, his defined shoulders where they shone in the outdoor tree-bulbs, wasn't helping.

"Uh, hey," I said nervously, setting the fruit back down. "I asked Corbin if it was okay."

He smiled, his eyes hidden by the back lighting from the kitchen. "Oh, it's fine. I know. I can't blame you, the pool is very relaxing. Mind if I join?"

I wasn't sure if I did, or didn't, want him in the pool with me. Sinking lower, letting my arms dip into the water, I calmed my voice. "It's your pool."

His grin was a bit toothy, his movements

graceful as he shut the doors and approached. Watching him move, I was reminded of how he had called my own motions 'beautiful' at the gallery. Compared to his natural grace, I was a damn klutz.

I wanted to say something, anything, to break the silence.

And then he took his shirt off.

It was a quick process, his fingers hooking at the hem, tugging it over his head. It was like watching something in slow motion. I'd known he was in shape, I could tell from his slim figure in his well fit clothing, but this...

His torso was solid, the body of a runner. A line led the way down his sternum, a path taking me on a journey of perfection. He was pale all over, but not unhealthy looking. Creamy white, I could pour him into a cup of coffee and take a deep drink.

He's way too sexy, dear lord. This is like some ridiculous cologne ad. When does the music start up?

Seth slid into the water, hardly making a sound. The pool wasn't gigantic, but it seemed even smaller as he crossed over to me. In the shallows, his eyes glinted. I was acutely aware of the fact I was only wearing a bikini.

He must work out twenty-four hours a day! Tensing with mild shame, I hugged myself under the water. I wasn't in awful shape, but when compared to this man, I felt like a flabby slob.

"Nice, right?" I blurted, looking for a topic to crack the tension.

"Yes," he agreed, leaning on the edge beside me. I thought, if he leaned over, our shoulders would touch. "So, how is the mural coming?"

"Oh, uh, good. I mean," I corrected myself, trying not to ogle his chest, "Slow. Sort of. I did the base setting, can't really do much actual painting till tomorrow."

"I see," he mused, looking upwards at the sky. It was cloudy, the only thing ruining this hilariously picturesque scenario. "Hmn. How early can you start tomorrow?"

I peeked at his face, studying his strong profile. "How early can Corbin pick me up?"

"As early as you need. But, like I said, you *can* stay the night." His gaze shifted back to me, unblinking. He froze me like a mouse about to be attacked by a snake, and the idea of being his prey made me shiver.

I whispered, "I know. Maybe another time. I think tonight I'll go home."

He nodded, then closed his eyes, sinking deeper into the pool until it brushed his chin. I joined him, letting it tickle my ears.

For some time, we drifted in silence.

I was awash in both the water, and my thoughts. *I still don't think I'm getting the whole picture here. This guy doesn't seem to be married, but he's rolling in money and might as well be a fitness model.*

I don't even know how old he is, late twenties? Either way, guys like this aren't single.

Not unless they have some sort of terrible history, or habits.

Also, why do I even care if he's available!?

Shooting a covert look at Seth's peaceful and dashing face, I endured a flash of frustration. *This is insane. He's essentially my boss, plus, I don't have a chance with him. He likes my art, that's all.*

Isn't it?

The kitchen doors slid open, a shadow casting onto both of us. Looking up, I saw Corbin standing there, a pair of towels in his hands. "Excuse me, but dinner is ready if you two are hungry."

I glanced at the plate of strawberries, blushing red as a beet. "I'm actually full. Honestly, would you mind taking me home, Corbin? I could use some rest."

And my poor hormones could use a break.

"That's a good idea." Seth pulled himself

from the pool, water rushing down every inch of his hard figure. I knew I was gawking, so I yanked my eyes away, wondering if either of the men had noticed.

He reached down, offering his hand. On reflex, I let him help me out of the pool. For a moment we bumped together, my knees wobbling. "Ah, sorry!" Stumbling back, I held my hands up—as if to keep him away.

His smile burned as strong as ever. If I had to guess, he wasn't affected by my nearness the way I was to his.

Dripping wet in my bikini, I hurried to grab the towel from Corbin, wrapping it around myself. Seth took the other towel, rubbing gently at his hair. The ruffled look worked for him.

Dammit, did any look *not* work for him?

"Well, Ms. Starling." He bowed his head. "It was a pleasure, I'll see you tomorrow."

I smiled. "Right, tomorrow." Looking down at my wet feet, I padded on them across the kitchen floor. Hurrying upstairs, I changed quickly, not wanting to make anyone wait around.

When I returned, the pair of men were talking softly by the front door. They stopped as soon as they spotted me descending the stairs.

"Goodnight, Seth." I waved, unsure if I

should shake his hand or not. *Ugh, I'm so awkward.*

He inclined his head, vanishing into the kitchen. As he went, I caught myself staring at his naked, broad shoulders, his waist still wrapped in the towel.

Corbin cleared his throat. I whipped my head around, and he opened the front door. "Shall we?"

With heat blooming up my neck, I chased him out to the car.

The drive back was just as lovely at night, the city below lit up like a sea of fireflies. It was faster as well, traffic no longer congested.

We pulled up outside of my apartment, and I slid out once Corbin opened my door. Opening my mouth, I started to say goodbye, but he stopped me when he offered a thick packet of papers.

"Oh." I blinked, taking them carefully. "My copy of the contract. Thanks."

"Mr. Hart asked me to give you that. He wanted me to remind you to read over the rules."

Scowling like I'd been chided, I lifted my chin. "Fine. Could you remind *him* that he'd be better received if he made a summary of this dictionary?"

Corbin chuckled. "Good night, Ms.

Starling. See you early in the morning."

I gave a slight wave, watching him drive off quietly into the night.

In my hands, the contract was as heavy as a cement block.

- Chapter Five -
Naomi

As promised, Corbin came early in the morning.

And, unlike *I* had promised, I hadn't read the contract at all. Initially, I'd been too irritated to. When that feeling had passed, I'd been flat out exhausted. I'd slept until my alarm blared at me, the contract used as a pillow.

Yawning, I stumbled into the car.

"Rough night?" Corbin asked. He handed me a cup of coffee, and I flared with gratefulness.

"Thank you!" Sipping it, I sank low in the car seat. "And not rough, not exactly." My dreams had been plagued by blue eyes and rock hard abs, but that hadn't been so bad. "I haven't spent so long on my feet in some time. Between the gallery and this, I guess the exertion is catching up with me."

"Make sure to eat well, and drink water," he said sagely.

Pursing my lips, I drank loudly from the coffee and smiled. "Yes sir."

Corbin dropped me off, saying he had errands. I waved after him, tossing the coffee cup in a small trash bin by the garage. I felt invigorated, ready to begin my day.

Seth was ready to remind me of why my dreams had been so strange.

He stood by the couches inside, his figure standing out in crisp slacks and a pale blue suit. He could have been waiting to do a photo-shoot for a magazine.

"Ms. Hart," he said. "Morning."

"Oh, morning," I said, scrambling to make conversation.

Lucky me, Seth had a topic at the ready.

"The contract. Did you read it over?"

Not wanting to lie, and consoling my guilt by deciding to read the contract later, I gave my most sincere smile and exclaimed, "Of course I read it!"

He didn't inquire further.

With a brisk now, he spun around, heading down a hall. "Then I'll leave you to it."

I didn't see Seth for some time, after that.

Setting up my gear, I tied my hair back and began painting. I had a lot of work ahead of me, I needed to get going.

Sometime into starting the first splotches of color, the tiny hairs lifted on the back of my neck. Turning, I noticed Seth standing in the foyer below.

His blue eyes were fixed hotly on me.

My stomach did a dive. *Why is he watching me, does he think I'll make a mistake?*

"Did you need something?" I called out.

Cocking his head, the man shrugged. "Not at all."

Hesitating, I debated probing further. This was very much like the time in the gallery. He'd crept up on me, watching me work... telling me I was graceful or beautiful or whatever...

Trying to ignore him, I focused on my art.

Greens melted into yellows, blacks danced with reds, the colors starting to blend and form the vague hint of what was in my head. The longer I kept at it, the easier it was to forget my audience. Eventually, I was only aware of my own motions.

I lived art, breathed art, my body twisting as it made wide swatches or dainty details. This was my craft, this was what I loved, and it came out in the results.

How long Seth watched me, I couldn't say. When I took a quick glance over my shoulder, some hours later, he'd disappeared. It should have made me glad. Strangely, instead, I endured the sour tang of disappointment.

Wanting my boss to ogle me as I worked was... wrong.

Very wrong.

Setting my shoulders, I went back to painting. It was the only thing I had to distract me from the warm desire that craved more attention from that handsome, mysterious man.

Focus, focus, focus.

I had to stop thinking about Seth. I had to get a damn grip on my mind and my emotions and just... just...

The doorbell blasted throughout the mansion, ripping me from my reverie. Jerking around, confused, I watched below as someone moved towards the front door. It wasn't Seth, I realized, but Corbin.

I looked on as the chauffeur opened the door. Outside, I could see the blue hue of evening. How long had I been working for?

Then *they* entered, and I stopped caring about the time.

Silver and smoke, the pair was clad head to toe in expensive formal wear. On their faces were masks, hiding their expressions and identities. I was sure I wouldn't have known them, anyway.

Corbin bowed his head, then motioned them inside. I leaned on the railing, curiosity bubbling hot. Together, the three of them

68

approached the gold door below the winding staircase. I covered my mouth when Corbin opened it.

Just like that, the strangers were gone.

Corbin looked up at me, as if silently daring me to speak. Biting my tongue, I turned away nervously, trying to decide what to make of this.

Who were those people, and why did they go in that door? What's down there?

Lifting my paintbrush, I did my best to ignore the situation.

The doorbell rang again.

Trying to be sly, I peered with one eye as I worked. Corbin was letting in a new group, this time consisting of five people. As before, they were dressed nicely, but their masks hid who they might be. I could tell some were women, but that was all.

Escorted to that alluring door, they vanished behind it in silence. Corbin didn't bother glancing at me, but I assumed he knew I was staring.

This is strange, is there a party going on I didn't know about?

Frowning in thought, I squinted at the wall. It was too difficult to focus, especially as the guests began arriving faster and faster. Soon, I abandoned all pretense, just standing by the rail to watch.

One of the visitors, a man in a black mask, looked my way. His lips coiled into a smirk below that shining mask, an expression that made my heart throb. It was the sort of look that *promised* things. I couldn't see his eyes, but I imagined they were smoldering.

And then, like the rest, he was gone.

Eventually, no more came, and Corbin vanished from the main room. Alone, nothing guarding me from that strange door, my blood began racing. I was warm with excitement, wanting so badly to run down the stairs, to just *look* beyond that secret portal.

Eyeballing my paint stained jeans and messy shirt, I wrinkled my nose. *I can't risk looking inside, and I'm obviously out of place. What if someone saw me?* I shivered at the concept.

What if Seth found out?

Tapping my cheek, I sighed. There was simply no way to manage it, how could I even attempt it?

Will Corbin tell Seth I was spying?

I didn't think so, but it was possible. Was there a 'rule' about not watching people when they arrived? I nearly rolled my eyes.

Honestly, I was exhausted, and my thoughts roamed towards home. But facing Corbin now was... too much. Imagining his accusing eyes, I wandered down the hall to the guest room.

Flicking on the light, I glanced around. I'd been inside briefly last night, but hadn't probed too deep.

The bed was large, the blankets creamy. Few things could be so tempting when you're tired. I wasn't set on sleeping here, but as I tested the plush bed, discovered the private bathroom... my resistance was waning.

It would be nice to be able to sleep here, I'd get to wake up and paint at my leisure.

Kicking off my shoes, my attention wandered to the bureau where I had found the teal bikini. I studied the big closet, wondering if the contents could be even better.

The bed springs squeaked as I hopped to my feet. Gripping the carved handles, I peeled the double doors open. Inside, there were hangers upon hangers of different outfits.

Deeper, I found cupboards stuffed with shoes. Everything was brand name, high-end labels. There was jewelry stacked in layers on various small 'tree' shaped units.

Gaping, I stepped further in, finding the dangling chain of a light bulb. Illuminated, the space seemed even wider, like a warehouse of a wardrobe.

Touching the soft dresses, silk tops, comfortable fitness wear, I started laughing.

Amazing. All this, just sitting here?

Opening some drawers, I continued to find intriguing items. Bracelets, hats, sunglasses, there was even makeup. It boggled the mind. I almost stepped out, my skin tingling with unease.

Why keep all this, what's the point?

Then, my eyes fell on a chest in the corner.

Curious, for how could I not be, I crouched down and brushed my hand over the surface. It didn't seem old, but who kept things like elaborate chests around? *Maybe there's treasure inside.* Seth the pirate, what an idea.

Gingerly, I popped the lid.

I was right.

Treasure *was* waiting for me.

It was exactly what I had been looking for, though I hadn't realized it. Dipping my arms into the chest, I pulled out the most perfect of finds.

An ornate mask.

****

It was a risk, I knew that.

I knew it in my trembling skin, and deep down in my bones.

If Seth finds out, I don't want to know what he'll do. I could be risking more than my admission into college.

Despite this, I slipped out of the guest room. Below the railing, I saw no one, not even Corbin. The gold door was closed, calling to me with the promise of secrets...

And answers.

It was good that no one was around. In my current ensemble, I would have been startlingly obvious.

Black velvet down to my ankles, strapless and smooth, the dress hugged every inch I had. I'd picked it based on what the people coming into the mansion had been wearing. I'd seen only dark colors.

My shoes were basic flats, in case I needed to run.

I'd also wrapped my hair up and out of the way, exposing the back of my pale neck. I'd tried to imagine what someone might recognize about me. I didn't wear my hair in any elaborate style in my day to day life.

Most of all, though, I hoped the mask would divert any suspicion.

It was ornate, covered in opals that I thought were too big to be real. Pure white, it was beyond gorgeous. It covered everything from my forehead to my nose.

I'd spread some gloss over my lips, but most of it was gone; chewed away by my nervous teeth.

Glancing side to side, like I was in some over the top spy movie, I scurried down the stairs. It was a fast process, so fast it left me dizzy. Was success so simple? No one was going to walk into the room at the last second and stop me?

My palm curled around the handle, touching the gold door for the first time. With one last, solid inhale of air, I tugged on the brass knob. Quickly I stepped inside, shutting the door behind me. I barely held back a laugh of relief.

Breaking the rules had given me a mild euphoria. It wasn't like me to be so bold, but...

But I did it, and it feels good.

I was standing at the top of a set of stairs, illuminated by orange lamps along the walls. The ceiling was low, and because the walls curved, I couldn't see what was at the bottom.

Well, I've come this far.

Swallowing, I began my descent. The stairs were carpeted, yellow and earthy, the walls a shade darker. It wasn't a long walk, opening into a small room below. Here, there was a set of heavy purple curtains over an archway. A small table waited on the left, clipboard resting on top.

Pausing beside it, I read what was clearly a list of names. Was this a sign-in sheet of sorts? Running a finger down the page, I didn't recognize anyone. Quickly, it became obvious why.

These can't be real names, can they? 'Scarlet,' 'Fang,' 'Helm?' What is going on down here?

Distantly, through the curtains, I could hear the soft pulse of music... and voices.

Frowning, I abandoned the list. Carefully, I brushed the curtains aside; a small crack, just enough so I could peer through.

There, I had my first glimpse of what was beneath Seth's mansion.

What I saw left me speechless.

- Chapter Six -
Naomi

It was a large room, wide and with other alcoves leading off to who knew where. Dark inside, the only light sources were a few candles here and there. It gave everything a sinister aura which, as I looked on, was all too fitting.

People stood around, talking to each other softly. If I hadn't looked twice, it would have been innocuous. But there, at the feet of many of them, there were figures kneeling. Why would people *kneel* at the feet of others?

Everyone still wore their masks, which calmed me some, but the situation was nerve wracking. What kind of party was this? What the hell had Seth organized down here?

Had he organized this?

Fidgeting, I wondered what I should do. *If I turn and leave, no one will know.* I'd gone unnoticed, the attendees too involved to give me more than a glance. As I debated backing out, my curiosity partially sated, a sound reached me from one of the archways.

It was a raw noise; animal in nature. It sent a tingle down my spine, my lower belly twitching.

I knew what that sound was.

It wasn't even a question.

That's a woman moaning, but... why?

The noise came again, a groan full of pleasure and passion. My own body heated up, just from hearing it. Around me, no one else reacted. Their calmness piqued my interest further. Did women usually sob in obscene delight down here?

I wanted to know what was making someone create such openly erotic noises.

Just a peek at what's further inside, then I'll leave.

Calming my nerves, grateful for the mask that hid my blushing cheeks, I stepped deeper into the room. No one acted like I wasn't welcome; that was encouraging.

Just one foot in front of the other.

I glanced down as I passed one of the couples. The man had his hand on the woman's head, his fingers casually petting her long hair as he spoke to another fellow standing nearby. The lady seemed to be enjoying it, leaning into the touch with a smile on her lips.

Another moan floated down the hall, my skin rippling in reaction.

Whatever is going on, she sounds like she's enjoying it.

I rounded the passage, walking the short

length of the dimly lit corridor. There, at the end, another archway waited, its curtains spread open.

My steps slowed as I grew near, the fact that I was about to get answers making me wary. My ribs creaked with the giant swell of air I took in.

Just do it!

Crossing the threshold, I saw the source of the noise.

My knees locked up instantly.

A woman was bent over a large table, her legs spread, muscles tense and shaking. Sweat coated her thighs, her perfectly shaped ass pointed into the air. She was naked, breasts crushed beneath her on the hard surface, arms pulled forward and bound at the wrists.

Her ankles were tied to the legs of the table, a position that exposed her glistening pussy to any eyes around.

And there were *many* eyes.

Biting my tongue to hold my gasp at bay, I scanned the people. Some stood, like me, arms folded or hands gripping drinks. Others were lounging comfortably on luxurious couches. Men, women, it didn't matter who they were...

All of them were watching.

On one wall, I saw another woman, her

78

body taut where she was strapped and spread in tight looking bonds. A robe ran down her torso, winding between her breasts and highlighting their shape. From how she wiggled, it looked like she was enjoying herself.

Everything I looked at could have come straight from some perverse BDSM catalog. I'd been on the internet, I wasn't so naïve that I couldn't say what this reminded me of.

Leather, bondage, power and fantasy...

Then, I saw *him*.

The man who'd smiled at me when he'd entered the house.

A vision of muscle and stoic silence, the man stood against the wall across from me. Wearing entirely all black, I hadn't noticed him initially with the dim lighting. He had on crisp pants, a thick belt. That perfect torso was exposed in detailed glory, shirt unbuttoned down the front. His hands were clad in glossy, deep-smoke gloves.

The stranger's stance, his aura, it was intimidating. I was glad he wore a mask like all the others. I worried that if I had seen his eyes, they'd make my insides melt.

Who is that?

My ogling ended; loud footsteps announced a new man.

His golden mask gazed over all of us, but his focus was on the woman tied to the table.

Only she held his true attention.

The man's body language spoke for him, making it clear he was solely focused on her. His head tilted down, eyes gliding from her ankles to her bare back.

The gold-masked stranger stepped forward, standing behind the prone woman who gave a soft whimper. Her blonde hair was in disarray, it hid her face when she tried to peek over her shoulder.

"Don't look," he spat, his tone icy.

That severity made the woman obey, and... it made my pussy throb. I don't know why I reacted so strongly. Never in my life had I seen such a casual display of dominance.

I must have let out a tiny noise, because the man in black across from me glanced my way. His slight smile was a distraction all its own. I caught a hint of porcelain teeth, his cocky amusement thrilling me the same way the gold-masked-man's voice had.

Gold-Mask's hand came down, brushing along the woman's lower back, tracing the curve of one ass cheek. Instantly, she moaned, and I bit my lower lip harder. It felt wrong, watching this display, but everyone in the room was just as entranced.

Even the stoic man in black was craning forward, his arms taut over his chest.

Stepping between the blonde's thighs,

cupping her rear, Gold-Mask—as I'd begun thinking of him—spread her pliant flesh. He exposed her slick, pink folds.

When he chuckled, my core tightened. "You're so wet, little pet. Why would that be? Do you like everyone watching you like this, showing them all how much you *need* to be punished?"

Punished?

The blonde whimpered, then again when the man slapped her ass hard enough to leave a red mark. "Answer me, girl."

"Yes!" she sobbed, arching her spine to get more of his touch. "Yes, Master!"

Master.

I was stunned. My body was thrilling with anticipation over the whole scene. Her words sealed it; my slow boiling suspicion was right. I *knew* what was happening here. There was no other explanation for this over the top scene.

But... why would Seth Hart allow a sex party down here?

What kind of a man *was* he?

"Always answer your Master when they ask you a question, girl. Your mistakes reveal why you're here, why you need training." Gently, he ran a finger between the gap of her thighs. I was sure he must have touched her slit, because she moaned louder than before.

81

"Would you like me to fuck you? It sounds like you want that."

"Yes, yes Master, oh god, please!" Squealing, she gyrated her hips. My own pussy quivered in sympathy.

"Well," the man she'd called Master whispered, so that I leaned forward to hear better, "Then beg for it. Promise you'll be a good pet and obey your Master from this moment on. Always." His thumbs peeled her pussy open, vulgarly displaying her twitching clit. "And forever."

I licked my mouth, far too warm from watching this scene. I saw that one of the men sitting down on a plush couch had his legs spread wide. Between them, a mop of brunette hair was moving. He was receiving a blow job, right there in the open.

No one batted an eye.

The man in black followed my eyes. Then, oddly, he stared at me once more. I didn't like that, it made me worry I was drawing attention to myself. Did I stand out that much?

Peering side to side, I frowned. *If I am, why is he the only one watching me?*

The wet sounds of the blow job made me flinch. At my hips, I clenched my hands roughly into fists. *This place is crazy! I should leave, just walk out and go.*

But I didn't.

"Please, sir, I'll do anything! I promise." The blonde sobbed, her hair tossing as she lost herself in her desperate need for release. "I'll always obey! Just please, please..."

"Good girl, that will do for now." Gold-Mask laughed, reaching down and rubbing the bulge in his pants.

After he drew attention to his erection, I couldn't look away. Staring, the insides of my thighs damp, the sight of that hand so casually outlining his own cock entranced me.

He freed it, the fleshy tip bouncing into the dim light. His hand, firmly gripping the base and giving it a slow pump, made me inhale audibly.

It was too much.

Finally, I looked away—and right at the black-masked guy across from me.

My observing stranger tilted his head. I realized he'd heard me gasp. For a moment, I was frozen with fear. My mind buzzed, warning me to turn and run, that something awful was about to happen. Perhaps my cover would be blown, or worse.

Soundlessly, he looked back to the bound woman and the other man.

I breathed out in relief. *He doesn't care, why am I worried? Everyone else is watching. I'm fine, I don't stand out.*

The blonde woman panted loudly, unable to move enough to rock the Master's cock into her. It was clearly torture, being tied down and teased. Blood quickened in my veins when I helplessly imagined myself in a similar predicament.

Watching this is actually turning me on, what's wrong with me? I'd never been interested in this kind of kink before.

Long fingers curled into her mop of hair, pulling her head back. Her lips parted in a silent cry of delight. He crouched, whispering into her ear. I couldn't hear what was said, but I wished I had.

Whatever it was, it made the woman cry out, clear as a bell. "Yes! Yes Master, of course!"

With a slow thrust, his plump cock slid into her from behind. I wondered what that felt like, after being tormented for so long. To finally have such a hard length filling her completely. It had to feel amazing, right? So warm and thick and...

Wow, I need to calm down!

Reaching up, I wiped at the back of my neck. Every inch of me was alive, and still, my senses heightened more as I watched the pair fucking on the table. He moved with purpose, holding her jaw, talking or nibbling at her ear.

The blonde had no control, the one she

kept calling 'Master' was able to use her at his leisure. He chose the speed, the force, and the woman could only accept what he gave.

I resisted a lusty hiss between my teeth when he abruptly rocked his hips, burying himself in the woman so hard the impact of flesh rang in the room.

Shifting anxiously, I squeezed my knees. My panties were soaked.

Again and again, he held her down and fucked her. Finally, he reached back between her legs with his slippery fingers. The way the woman squealed, I was positive he'd started rubbing her clit.

My mind was on a ride.

I pictured being bent over, made to scream in front of all these people; a strong man casually fucking me... teasing me towards the pressure of release...

I wonder how that woman got into this situation?

Suddenly, the blonde screamed, a hoarse sound that betrayed what had happened. Her thighs quivered, then they grew weak. Gold-Mask thrust into her a few more times, letting her hair go so her head could rest on the table.

She came, didn't she? I just watched her, everyone watched her!

My belly fluttered, flesh prickling with a

growing ache. Watching the man, his arms flexing, his rhythm slowing, I was confused when he suddenly pulled free. His cock, hard and angry in the air, was coiled in his fist.

Rapidly, he jerked his own length. The explosion of pearly liquid hit the woman's ass, coating her skin and dripping down. Standing there, he rubbed the slippery head of his cock on her hip, then tucked it away in his trousers.

With one more final, crisp slap on her thigh, he turned towards us and smiled. "Cora, clean her up and untie her. Make arrangements for her auction."

"Yes, Master." A woman, her hair in a woven, raven braid, offered him a glass of water and a small towel. She began unbinding the blonde, washing her skin as she did so.

The room rumbled to life, everyone starting to move around and talk. It was like a spell had been broken, it reminded me of a crowd after a movie had ended.

Turning my head, I breathed in a few times to try and relax. That scene had been intense, I could never have imagined such a thing existing behind the golden door above.

Someone moved near me, people bustling to exit down the tunnel. I was jostled, so I mumbled a quick apology. As I twisted back around, I found myself face to face with the man who'd been watching me from the wall.

His voice was smooth as smoke. "Hello there, I don't believe we've met. Are you new?"

Oh, shit. "Um, uh," I sputtered, wishing I could melt into the crowd and escape. "I... yes, this is my first time here."

"I thought so." He grinned. "Normally, everyone should arrive in the main room at the start of the night. Late comers are discouraged." He was chiding me, but he didn't seem upset. Inclining his head, he gave me a once over. "I'm Master Onyx, and you are...?"

Fuck fuck dammit make something up!

"Opal," I blurted, thinking about my mask. I forced a smile, hoping he would go along with my lies.

He paused, taking a drink from a woman passing by with a tray. She bowed her head, but when she offered me a glass, I didn't take it. "Opal, that's nice. This is your first time, you said? What about this place brought you here? Curiosity?"

"Actually, sort of, yes." *Guess I don't need to lie about everything.*

"Then, did you see enough tonight to help you decide which path you'll choose?"

He was losing me. I hesitated, worried I would give myself away if I revealed my lack of knowledge. "I'm not sure. What path did you choose?"

"Isn't it obvious?" He laughed, like I'd made a great joke. Flexing a gloved hand between us, the surface creaking, he bent closer. "The life of a Dom is not for everyone, but I knew right away. We have a few women who do it, but here, it's mostly the men."

A Dom? I wasn't intimately familiar with the title, but I could figure out his meaning from context. A Dom was a Master.

Master...

I'd forgotten to breathe; the air came out in a hot burst. His nearness, the reminder of the show we'd both watched, was making me flustered. "Aha, right, I see. So... the other choice is more common for women?"

"Indeed," he said. "Most become submissives. When you decide, there is a list at the door. Just sign your name on the correct page, indicating you'd like to begin your training." If I could have seen his gaze, I swear he would have winked. "I'd be happy to teach you what it means to bow to a Master, my pretty little Opal."

My mouth opened, but no sound came out. He was so tall, I could have been swallowed in his shadow. If I'd thought the gold-masked man was intense, Onyx put him to shame. He was a tornado of wickedness and turbulence, ready to claw me up.

Someone clapped him on the shoulder.

"Sir, Helm would like to talk to you."

Onyx frowned, but only for a second. Nodding his head to me, he turned—but his words were liquid silver on his tongue. "Think about what I said. I'd love to hear you gasping again... and from more than just watching a little show."

Then, he allowed himself to be led away.

I breathed out, hard, leaning on the wall to steady myself. *He really was paying attention to me earlier.* I was torn between being flattered and terrified. This whole night had been insane. I was ready to leave.

Spinning, I walked quickly from the room, heading out through the group of people gathered in the main area. None of them spoke to me, and I was grateful.

Shoving aside the heavy curtain, my eyes fell on the small table by the archway.

The clipboard, where people sign in... and make their choice.

Peering side to side, finding myself alone, I reached down and flipped through the papers. Now that I knew what I was looking for, it made more sense. These were lists, each of them labeled different things.

Here. I tapped one side. The top read 'New Subs.' *This is where he told me to sign.* There were only three names. I wondered if one of them had been the blonde I'd watched earlier.

I imagined what it would be like to sign my name there, to put down 'Opal' on that list.

Would I end up tied to a table, spanked and teased until I lost myself in bliss?

Would that man, Onyx, be the one to do it all to me?

If he really meant what he said, then... Trembling, I wrenched myself away and shook my head. *No, get a grip. This isn't for you.*

With one last look at the clipboard, I fled up the stairs.

- Chapter Seven -
Naomi

The paint smudged along the wall, long strokes of ebony, smokey and rich. Carefully, I added some loose swirls of yellow, creating a burst of contrast. It seemed abrupt, a spark of color from the darkness. I liked the effect.

Apparently, so did Seth.

"That's coming along nicely," he said from my left. Shocked, I spun, ocher paint splattering onto the man's dove-grey jacket.

"Seth! I'm so sorry!" Horrified, I reached for a rag, but he only lifted his hands and chuckled.

"Shh, easy! It's fine," he stated, studying the stain. "I didn't mean to scare you, I was just appreciating your work."

My expression smoothed, but I wasn't entirely convinced I hadn't just ruined an expensive outfit. Setting the brush down on my pallet, I put on a frail smile. "I'm seriously sorry. I shouldn't have freaked out. I'm just a little tired."

Seth squinted at me, like he was trying to figure out what I meant. I didn't like him being so interested.

"Well," he began, "I was going to talk to

you about that. You've been working very hard these past two days, I don't want you burning out with late hours."

Just like that, I was reminded of last night.

The cries of pleasure, sharp cracks from palms on smooth flesh; it sent a flicker of heat into my belly. *I'm not tired from painting all night, I'm tired because I couldn't sleep after...*

In my mind, I heard Onyx's voice, his promise.

'I'd be happy to teach you what it means...'

I shivered.

It had been impossible to decompress after everything I'd witnessed. I'd crawled into the guest bedroom, not even debating asking Corbin for a ride home. This morning, my sheets had been soaked in sweat. I'd been eager —more than eager—to get up and get to work to avoid thinking about why.

Seth was still talking. I shook my head, making myself pay attention.

"—for lunch. If that's alright."

"Wait, what?" I stared, wishing I'd heard everything he'd said.

"I mean, if you insist on not eating with me, I'll understand. But getting away from this wall might do you some good." His smile was gentle, his eyes melting over me.

He wants to have lunch?

It was so simple and innocent. I was flattered by his offer. "Sure, I'd like that. When do you want to do this?"

Laughing, he reached into his jacket. The pocket watch he pulled forth caught the light, glittering like an ocean of stars. "I was thinking now, actually."

"Now?"

"Ms. Starling, it's after two, didn't you realize?"

I hung my head, closing my eyes in defeat. *Where has my mind been all day?* It was a silly thing to ask myself.

I knew where it had been.

Black gloves, dark promises.

"Alright," I declared, putting on a firm grin. "Alright, fine, let's get lunch. These paint fumes are going to my head."

****

I was both surprised, and grateful, when we didn't go very far.

Sitting out in the backyard, we reclined under a large umbrella to hide from the angry sun. It was beautiful; the sky clean and clear, everything smelling of freshly mowed grass.

Corbin served us glasses of mojitos, trays of chilled tomato soup and small finger sandwiches. I felt exorbitantly fancy. Though I was enjoying the pampering, it would have been better with the paint stains on my clothes washed off.

He didn't bother to change his jacket, what does it matter?

Seth swirled the ice in his glass, mint leaves dancing inside. "You stayed the night here, Corbin tells me."

Sipping my drink, enjoying the sugar on the rim, I nodded.

What else did he tell you?

"How did you like it?" he asked.

"What, staying here?"

Those blue eyes peered at me through the shade, making me shift on my chair. "Yes, I'm hoping you enjoyed yourself. I'm more at ease when I feel like a real host."

I motioned with half a sandwich, indicating the table of food, then the yard around us. "Isn't this being enough of a host?"

"For most people," he chuckled, closing his eyes as he sipped the mojito.

"But not for you," I stated bluntly. The alcohol was strong, making me bolder. Seth gave me a hard, questioning look, but I didn't back down.

"Not for me," he agreed. "I admit, I like having some... impact on how my guests are doing."

I relaxed my tense shoulders and nibbled a sandwich. "You like being in control."

There, on his face, was a hint of displeasure. That odd, burning threat I'd encountered the day I'd asked about the golden door.

He was silent, his mouth a deep line, brows hooded over his piercing sapphires. My facade was cracking, the alcohol not enough to keep me pushing him.

"Maybe," he whispered. "Is that a problem for you?"

Swallowing my drink in one gulp, I tried to avoid responding. *Shit, I've made him angry. What was I thinking?* "No, not a problem, it's your home after all."

"Correct," Seth nodded. "My home, my rules." For awhile, he just studied me. Was he trying to figure out my thoughts? The concept was terrifying. "You did agree to them, you know."

"Yes, right, I know." I gazed absently at the sandwich in my hand, my appetite gone. All this talk of rules was cutting into my guilt. Going through that door was wrong. Was my glimpse at the sin behind it worth risking the future I craved?

I needed that admission letter.

Seth could never, *ever* know what I'd done. And no matter the temptation, I couldn't do it again. The risk was too great.

"As long as we understand each other, Ms. Starling."

"Of course," I whispered, looking at my reflection in the ice. "We understand each other perfectly."

****

I want to say I had better discipline.

It took me three nights until I dug the mask out again.

It hadn't been my plan. Or I told myself that. I didn't *want* to break the rules Seth had set. But, as I watched the last person enter the gold door, and as Corbin seemed to vanish off to wherever, I couldn't fight my urge.

Is it because I want to see Onyx again?

I buried that thought down deep. I had one tantalizing man infecting my life... I didn't need another.

I put on a dress of shimmering ink and low heels, my lips colored like rubies. The opal mask was my armor.

Then, when the coast was clear, I slipped through the door. The thrill of making it this far gave me confidence. Seth was hardly around, how would he ever catch me doing this?

This is dangerous... but only if he finds out.

And all I wanted was another little peek.

Was that so bad?

At the bottom of the stairs, I bumped into someone.

"Oh!" I gasped, startled and wide-eyed at my mistake. *Shit, I've fucked up!*

The person turned, her mouth friendly, eyes kind through large mask holes. "Careful, that last step can catch you by surprise. I've fallen before."

"Yes, good advice," I replied, painfully on edge. As I looked around, I noticed there were several people standing in line in front of the purple curtain. Someone stood by the table, a man with no mask at all. A man I knew.

Corbin.

In his normal chauffeur clothes, he watched as people signed their names on the clipboard. The line was dwindling fast, my panic becoming a hard thistle in my guts.

What do I do? Will he recognize me?

The woman in front of me carefully wrote her name on a page. "I'm a little nervous about tonight," she confided.

Corbin offered a kind smile. "Don't be, just enjoy yourself."

"Right," she giggled. "I just didn't think I'd go this far." With that, she brushed through the curtains, leaving me alone with someone who could bring my world crashing down.

He looked up at me, so I forced a careful smile onto my face. Clearing my throat, I grabbed the pen, trying to focus on the clipboard. Instead, I kept flicking my eyes up at him, everything blurring in my massive panic.

In a rush, my fingers shaking, I hastily signed one of the pages. It was a scrawled mess, but I'd been aware enough to write 'Opal' and not my real name.

Get it done, get away from him!

I dropped the pen, fingers cramping. I didn't see where it fell, I was too nervous to watch anything but his calm expression. With a wordless nod, I rushed through the curtains.

On the other side, I breathed easier. My skin was melting from the flush of adrenaline.

I don't think he knew it was me. How could he, with this mask?

Right. If he'd known, he'd have stopped me.

That gave me some solace.

The main room was busy, I was sure there were far more people here than last night.

Winding through the group, I observed the women, the men, trying to get a grasp on the social cues. Before I had time, a voice rang out over the crowd.

"Attention, everyone!"

Instantly, there was silence. I followed the stares, spotting someone standing by a hallway. He was tall, built like a Greek statue, and wore the familiar pair of black gloves that had kept me from sleeping.

That's Onyx.

"I have the list," he said firmly, waving some papers. "These girls will step forward and kneel by me." He pointed to the floor in front of him.

There was a pregnant pause, everyone waiting anxiously. I figured this must be an important moment, but I wasn't sure why.

In his elegant mask that revealed his delicious lips, Onyx grinned. "Good. The first girl is Tara!"

There was a pleased murmur. I watched as a woman with short, curly brown hair moved forward. Her hands were linked nervously, like she wasn't sure what to do with them. Onyx smiled at her, and she returned it weakly, kneeling down by his feet.

"Next, I need Roseli!"

A woman who challenged the black outfits—her long dress pale yellow and almost transparent—moved with confidence from the crowd. Gently, she folded to the floor, bowing her head obediently.

I blinked, turning to tap the woman beside me. "Excuse me, but what are they doing?"

The lady pursed her lips at me, then looked back to Onyx. "Ah, you've never seen the new girls get collected? Master Onyx is gathering all the women who signed up to be trained as submissives. It's always exciting to see who they'll be, so you'll know if you're interested when they're auctioned."

I clenched my teeth, afraid I'd say something foolish. *Girls being trained to be submissives.*

Slaves.

I didn't know how to feel. It was absurd... it was crazy...

It was exciting.

And what was this about an auction?

Onyx was still calling out names, he soon had four girls at his feet. Looking at the list, opening his mouth, he hesitated.

That slow smirk brushed my heart.

He lifted his head and looked out over the crowd, speaking with clear delight in his voice. "And the last girl I'm looking for, is *Opal*."

At first, hearing the name, I didn't register it as my own. Standing there blankly, I watched Onyx looking around, seeking the girl he had named. The crowd mumbled, a hushed noise, and he said it again.

"Opal?"

Like a punch to the temple, I was nauseous and stunned. *He just called me, why did he call me? How...*

The people around me moved, spreading apart in confusion. Onyx was frowning, a break in the crowd revealed me to him.

The second he recognized me, his voice went silky. "Opal, come here and kneel."

What do I do, what do I do?

Everyone was staring. My legs were waterlogged. I thought, if I took a step, I'd simply crumble. Maybe cracking into a million pieces was better than acknowledging the man staring at me.

He pointed with a gloved finger, his tone low and without negotiation. "Here. Now."

His voice was powerful, tugging at my most vulnerable places. Strangely, I was compelled. Was it from fear? Pressure? Curiosity? I didn't know, and I didn't have the power to think about it.

I began to move.

Pulled forward, I was suddenly standing

within reach of that magnificent man. Here, I was so close, I could almost see behind his mask. The eyes are the window to the soul, and in my terror, I desperately wanted to know what Onyx's soul looked like.

His fingers reached out, gripping my jaw tightly. His words were low, cutting. "I was hoping you'd be on this list. I'm disappointed, though, that you seem to be *terrible* at obeying."

Obeying.

That simple word made my lashes flutter. How could this arouse me so much? It was as if I didn't know myself. This skin I wore was another person, a woman tempted by perverse things, a woman flush with dark desire.

Not me.

Not Naomi.

Onyx let his fingers drift, cupping my cheek. Each fraction of me that he touched turned to butter, burned to life. He whispered, "We have a lot of work to do. Now, kneel."

Then he let go, cold air forming between us. Released from his grip, my strength gave out. I fell weakly to my knees at his feet. My head hung, ears thumping with the drums of my incessant panic.

I was never supposed to be here. I'd just wanted to know more about this world, a place that Seth had tried to hide from me.

Now I was kneeling at the feet of a Master.

What have I gotten myself into?

- Chapter Eight -
Naomi

I walked with the group down a hallway. Like the other passages, it was dimly lit, but I could see where I was going. It was long, curving here and there. I was positive we were traveling deeper.

Behind me and the other girls, a trio of men walked. At the head of our parade was Onyx. He led the group, not speaking a word. The only sounds were our heavy steps, and the blood pounding in my temples.

What am I doing, I can't become a part of this, can I?

I had to admit, there was a slice of me—a small, tingling spark that made my heart pulse —that wanted to know what was going to happen.

And why was I scared?

This whole place was just some kind of sex game. If it got too intense, I could just leave.

If I want to leave, that is. I shuddered. *Stop it. This is insane.*

I shouldn't have been getting worked up, but I was.

I was thinking about the blonde woman.

The gold-masked man had taken her into a realm of pleasure I'd never seen. My belly quivered at the idea of getting to experience being tied down... to be dominated by someone so confident, so powerful...

Someone like Onyx.

Lifting my eyes, I peeked over the shoulder of the woman in front of me, the one in the yellow dress. *Her name was Rose or something, Roseli?*

Squinting, I focused on the stiff, broad shoulders of the Master at the head of the procession. Studying the back of his skull, the dark hair that the mask couldn't hide, I didn't notice he had stopped moving until I bumped into the other woman.

Roseli shot a scowl my way. Blushing, I tried to communicated an apology without speaking.

Onyx spun, his hand reaching out to touch the handle of a heavy door, this one tan and aged. "Listen to me. When you enter this place, there is no turning back."

Does that mean, if I want to leave, it has to be now? Before we go inside?

The idea was appealing, but I was too terrified to speak up, or to even try and wiggle past the men behind me. No one else was moving, the other women didn't seem ready to bolt.

105

That's because they were prepared for this, I thought sullenly.

"Your training starts behind here, and from then on, you will be changed," he said. "When you return here, you will never be anything more than a submissive—a slave."

A slave. My lungs shivered.

"Keep that in mind," he went on. "There will be no more cavorting around this dungeon. You will do as you are told, you will become property." His eyes fell on me, then, staring at me through the sharp shadows.

As if he were talking directly to me, he said softly, "This is not something to take lightly. If you stay, I promise you... a part of you will never leave. It will always be tied up in this place."

I hugged myself to control the shaking that had started in my bones. *I wonder what that means?*

"Now." He smiled. "Let us begin."

The door was opened, and everyone followed Onyx inside. My turn arrived, and my heels dug in. The chance at escape was tempting me.

All I had to do was back away.

Why didn't I back away?

Stepping through, I glanced around, confused by what appeared to be a simple room with couches and chests. There were doors all along the walls, I resisted the urge to ask where they went.

Onyx ushered us girls into the center, then turned and whispered to the three other men. Uneasily, I watched them talking, wishing I could hear the words being exchanged.

"Roseli," Onyx called out, and the woman straightened. "You'll be working with Master Jack." He gestured to a man who wore a grinning wolf mask, his arms folded calmly. She made no argument, though I noticed how her lips curled down at the edges.

Had she wanted to go with someone else?

"Tara, you're with Master Helm."

As he went down the line, I experienced a sense of dread blooming. *Who am I going to end up with?* I knew who I wanted, but admitting it was shameful. I didn't even dare to bring up his promise to me.

Finally, as the last of the woman were paired off, that dark man in all his devilish glory turned to face me. "And you, my lovely Opal... You'll be with me, of course."

Of course.

The flicker of pleasure hit me hard. I couldn't mute my relieved smile. If I was going to indulge in this, I wanted it to be with Onyx. I wasn't sure why, but a part of me felt like I could trust him.

Like I already knew him, somehow.

He motioned to me, and I came forward, following him to a door in the wall. "You'll all go with your Masters and be sequestered for your training."

I'm going to be alone with him!

That knowledge was overwhelming. I needed something to quench my parched throat, or to soak up the welling arousal in my core. One realization sobered everything.

He called himself my Master. That feels... wrong.

With one more glance over at the other women, their figures vanishing into various exits, I looked back up at Onyx.

The man radiated an aura of command, but I didn't think of him as *my* Master. I didn't think of anyone like that. This underground world was sexy, and decadent, but as much as he claimed this would change me...

I knew better.

I wasn't a slave. Onyx couldn't break me.

Calmed by my rationalization, I followed him through the door.

****

Everything was dark, a velvety orange. I

gazed around, noting everything, but mostly the silence. *I'm really alone with him.* To say I was having second thoughts about this was putting it mildly.

The room had soft carpet, smooth walls. It was decorated with various devices, all of which made my heart beat faster.

Chains hung from the ceiling, or were bolted to the floor. In one corner, I saw a glass shower. It disturbed me to see something so normal. *Why is that even here? I don't think I want to know.*

The furniture was unique; padded and angled in ways that made it clear they were meant for devious purposes. Saw-horses, stocks, things I couldn't identify, they were everywhere.

He moved beside me, making me jump when his soft glove cupped my chin. Forcing my head up, Onyx looked into my face. I was grateful, again, for the mask.

"I'm pleased you decided to become a sub, Opal. Did you decide because of the show the other night?"

The memory of the blonde woman, begging and writhing, had me chewing my tongue.

"Or," he chuckled, "Did you choose after you spoke with me? Did I *intrigue* you?"

He's perceptive. And god, the way he

phrases things!

His fingers tightened, bordering on painful. "Answer me, girl."

"Y—yes, I—" That grip squeezed until I winced.

"No, address me correctly."

Correctly? What does he mean?

My mind churned, fighting the concoction of adrenaline and confusion. Finally, I pulled forth what I thought he wanted. "Yes, Master Onyx."

Calling him that made my stomach flip. It felt weird, the words heavy on my tongue.

Chuckling, he let me go. I rubbed my chin tenderly. "We have a lot of work to do. You've never done anything like this before, have you?"

"No," I admitted reluctantly, my eyes moving to the far wall. I was thrown off already, his flip between seduction and cruelty leaving me dizzy.

"Oh, don't worry." His hand reached out, fingers deftly tracing the line of my throat. That quick touch flared my arousal. He was keeping me on my toes. "I'm a very good teacher. You'll understand your role in no time."

I thought my heart might explode, my attention fixed on those perfect, smiling lips. They parted, and his tone was firm, unyielding.

"Now, kneel."

This still felt awkward, but after doing it earlier, my mind didn't battle it. Wordlessly, I knelt, though it wasn't graceful. My legs buckled, I grabbed at the ground to keep myself from landing on my face.

Onyx laughed, shaking his head at the display. "You'll need to get better at that, such a clumsy girl."

Blushing, I stared at his shiny boots, mentally agreeing. *Seth told me my movements were beautiful. Guess he was wrong.*

Onyx moved around me, a shark circling in the water. I tried not to think about it like that, but this man had so much control over me, I was at his mercy.

For a moment, he said nothing. The only sounds were his footsteps, muffled by the rug.

"You're lovely," he mumbled.

He touched the back of my skull, and I jerked, unable to keep calm at the intimate contact. Gently, he stroked the back of my neck until my skin was vibrating. The glove was luxurious, it sent sparks right into my brain cells.

Already warm, I was getting excited by this powerful man's touch. It was happening rapidly, my muscle coiling, seeking release from the build up I'd endured since the show with the blonde. "I... that..."

"Shh," he hissed, tightening his hold like I was a puppy gripped by the nape. "I didn't ask you anything. Don't talk without permission, or unless I've asked a question. Now, I'd like to see how lovely the rest of you is."

My insides became hard as rocks.

Onyx must have sensed my response, his fingers holding tight on my soft throat. "Stand, Opal."

I wasn't sure if I could, but I tried. Every bit of me was shaking, he ended up assisting me most of the way. Finally, I stood there, his chest grazing my spine. Onyx whispered, lips tickling my ear. "Take off your dress."

I can't, I'm not ready for that!

Trembling, I flexed my hands at my sides, but made no attempt to follow his order.

That was my first mistake, one that my 'new Master' was not keen to overlook.

"One more chance, or I'll do it for you."

I squeezed my eyes shut, willing myself away. *I can't, I can't,* I thought in a panic.

When Onyx sighed, he sounded disappointed. "So that's how it is."

Rough, fast, he grabbed me by the shoulders and spun me around. Squeaking, I gawked as he held my arms, pulling them over my head. Too stunned to struggle, not that it would have helped, I felt him binding my wrists quickly with something.

Rope, that's rope hanging from the ceiling.

It took seconds, leaving me amazed and distraught at his skill. Tugging at the restraints, fear began bubbling in my center. I was trapped, utterly at the mercy of someone I hardly knew.

What the hell was I thinking, this guy is a complete stranger! He could hurt me, why was I so reckless?

Onyx folded his arms, smiling as he looked me up and down. "There, much better."

"Let me go," I stuttered, knees wobbling. *If my legs give out, I guess I won't fall, at least.*

"You don't tell me what to do. Don't you understand that? You're here," he hissed, grabbing my jaw and forcing me to look at his scowl, "Because you asked for this. You *want* this, so don't mistake my commands as suggestions. I said undress, you did not. This..." He smirked, letting me go and gripping my wrists. "Is your punishment."

He's insane, I thought. *Or maybe I am, for following him down here.*

Languidly, he ran his fingers down my arms, bringing my goosebumps to a stiff point. He caressed my shoulders, then stroked down

113

my dress, following the line between the valley of my breasts.

The combination of silken clothing, and his firm touch, sent a jolt into my pussy.

What was that about? I'm in god damn danger, I can't be getting turned on over this!

Easily, he traced my sides, embracing the curve of my hips and chuckling. Onyx moved around me, but when I tried to follow him with my eyes, he grabbed the back of my head, twisting it back. "Don't look at me," he growled.

Panic morphed into feral anger. Gritting my teeth, I acted before I thought it through. One leg kicked out, catching him in the hip. "Untie me! Let me go! I don't want to do this anymore!"

Swirling fingers in my hair, he yanked my neck into an arch. I could barely see his face. "You can't hold still, and you can't be quiet. This isn't a very good start for you, little slave."

Swallowing, I said, "Fuck you, I'm not a slave."

"No?" His laughter surprised me. He released me, but it was brief. I didn't know what he held, only that something firm was being shoved between my teeth, a strap fixed behind my head. The rubber flavor tainted my tongue.

Noise rose in my gullet, but the gag muffled me.

He'd actually *gagged* me!

Without my voice, I'd been robbed of the last bit of control I had. *No,* I thought quickly. *I have one more thing left.*

I had my mind.

Onyx couldn't control that.

Coming around, he folded his arms and faced me. "You think you're not a slave, that you're not meant to kneel and please your Master." He chuckled, a noise that stroked my inner thighs as good as his hand could have. "I'll have fun proving you wrong."

Bending down, he caught my ankles. Easily, he spread them wide, fixing them inside two straps bolted to the floor.

Oh god, oh god!

My chest was threatening to split open from the tremor in my lungs. I thought I'd been too deep before, but now, I knew what deep really meant.

"I'm going to break you," he whispered, circling behind me.

His voice coerced a wave of excitement. *No! Control yourself!*

I had to; it was all I could do.

Determined to bury the lust, I stared at the far wall, but it was torture of another kind, because I could see the exit. Once more, I tugged at the ropes, knowing it was hopeless. *I'm trapped, what will he do to me?*

Hands moved down my back, then further, cupping my ass cheeks, fondling them lightly. My shout was a mere mumble behind the gag. I started to writhe, shaking in my bonds.

He slapped my ass, the noise cutting the air. The pain traveled in a burst through my flesh, down to my toes.

"Clearly, you have trouble obeying. Let's fix that."

Wondering how he meant to 'fix' me, I flooded with worry.

And also with something else.

My whole core was electric. It burned inside of me, making my breathing heavier.

Don't give in to this, I demanded.

But with what he had planned... nothing I did would make a difference.

He'd said he was going to break me.

And he meant it.

Onyx crouched, gripping the hem of my dress to hike it up to my waist. The firm globes of my ass, clad tightly in black panties and red from the slap, were exposed to his eyes.

Knowing he could see so much, I struggled to get free, humiliated by being displayed.

"Hold still," he grunted, "Or this will be much worse."

Biting into the gag, I squeezed my fists above my head.

His hand made a path down the back of my thigh, feeling my tight muscles. They were straining, resisting the urge to fight. One whole palm cupped my ass cheek, gently testing how pliant it was. "Lovely," he murmured, inhaling slowly as if to calm himself.

I felt a confusing thrill, pleased that he found my body appealing.

Onyx stepped back, leaving me alone.

Where is he going?

His touch was gone, disappointment in its wake. My flesh was betraying me. I was losing the last bit of control I had. Even now, I was aching for him.

When he returned, it wasn't with the sweet caress of before. Utilizing his strong muscles, the body I so admired, he slapped me on the ass savagely.

"Mmf!" I groaned, the pain just barely worse than the indignity. Again, he brought his palm down, filling the air with thunder.

I was rattled, I had no idea how to handle this. *He's actually spanking me!*

"Slaves who don't follow directions need

to be punished. You must understand what you'll face if you try to resist, my dear." Lightly, he traced his fingers over my crimson skin, making me wince.

As he kept at it, the welts began to tingle.

It was like my skin was waking up, the sharpness melting into heightened strokes. Intrigued, and enjoying it in contrast to the slaps, I shut my eyes. *Why is that so nice?*

His hands brushed lower, catching the smooth inner part of my thigh. It was a quick contact, leaving soon enough, but it made my pussy twitch.

Shivering, my body embraced the sudden pleasure after the torture. The skin on my ass was pulsing as the blood spread back where it belonged, and my cunt seemed to follow the rhythm with a sympathetic beat of its own.

Abruptly, Onyx halted his ministrations, leaving me unprepared for another round of spanking. This time, angry tears welled up. *I want him to stop!* I jerked in the ropes, wishing I could will him with my wet eyes.

Through the red bursts of pain, I noticed how quickly I'd broken down. Was I so weak?

His fingers wrenched in my gag, pulling it from my sore jaw. Against my temple, he growled. "Promise me you won't disobey." He gripped my raw cheeks, giving a hard squeeze.

Gasping, my tongue was sluggish— speaking was a chore. *This is it, I can tell him what I think of all this.*

I could call him a monster.

I could scream until my throat was bloody.

Onyx stroked his palms over my tender flesh, reminding me of what he could do to me.

Both good... and bad.

Like a shoddy dam, I broke. "Please, no more. I'll do what you say!"

"Promise me *correctly*," he admonished, dragging his nails over the pink marks shaped like his own hands on my milky skin.

Correctly, what does he mean?

Then I realized.

Ashamed by the words I had to speak, I pressed on desperately. "Master, I won't disobey! I promise I'll listen to you, so please..."

Chuckling, he let my dress fall back down, the silk cool on my sweltering body. "And the breaking begins. Alright, since you begged so pretty, I'll stop. Remember this, though," he said, moving around to stand before me.

Carefully, he lifted my head, gently brushing the tears off of my face. He was so close we could have kissed. "I was being very

119

kind. This was the most gentle of punishments. Next time, I will not be so patient. Do you understand, Opal?"

My heart pounded, body confused by the storm of sensations. I was hot as an ember all over, his touch and his words acted like oxygen to make me glow. "Yes," I breathed out in a rush. "I understand, Master. Thank you."

"Good girl." He smiled, and dammit, my ripple of delight was because I had pleased him again. Onyx was winning this game. It wasn't fair, he had more practice. He knew what to do, and I was just learning that my own body could betray me.

"Now, let's start over," he purred. His hands, agile as a thief's, untied the ropes above.

I grimaced at how tight my shoulders were, but I lowered my arms to my sides in relief. Onyx considered me, his hands folding behind his back. "Undress for me. This time, don't resist, I'd hate to think you learned nothing from what I showed you just now."

Yes, that's right. I couldn't get naked when asked, and so he did all of this.

Again, my chance to run had arrived.

Onyx was fast, but if I made it clear I wasn't playing around, he'd have to let me leave. Right? Wasn't this a game, dark as it was? No one could *really* be a slave, it wasn't possible.

Just a game...

My ass throbbed, but as I shifted, I realized my thighs were slick. His spanking had hurt, but there was no denying how excited it had made me.

He's dangerous! I need to run!

Peering at his confident smile, I hesitated.

And that was enough.

Taking a long, deep breath to steel my nerves, I reached for the clasp on my dress. I released the strings, the luscious gown falling down like rain. It pooled around my feet, leaving me standing before the masked man in only my lingerie.

No, I'm also masked. I can be brave about this if I consider that he doesn't know who I am. We're protected by being anonymous.

It didn't help entirely, but it was enough to keep my courage strong so I didn't cover myself and try to bolt.

Onyx tilted his head, eyeing me like I was a piece of art. That moment tickled me, reminding me of Seth—how he would watch me paint. I didn't want to compare the two men, but they were similar, weren't they?

For the first time, I felt a flash of guilt. Was this wrong of me? Doing this with Onyx? I'd been fawning over Seth for days. Was I so fickle?

"Turn for me," he commanded. Lifting my head, I did as he said. "I admit, you're very beautiful. But I think you look even better covered in my marks."

My face flushed to my hairline. I glanced back at him, having trouble meeting his eyes.

Does he really think I'm beautiful?

"Now, hold still," he said, stepping forward. I could smell him; it was a strong scent, like honey and olive oil. It made my head swim. I shut my eyes with a sigh.

His fingers came, gloved tips feeling my shoulders, sliding down and around to unclasp my bra. Knowing what was about to happen, my tendons stretched, on the verge of snapping. I was worried I might hit him again, just on instinct.

Relax. Don't be so scared, I told myself.

In the dim light, my breasts were revealed. His proximity had turned their tips firm. My dusky nipples were sensitive in the air, I inhaled on reflex.

"Lovely," he laughed. "I'm so pleased I picked you."

I smiled helplessly, opening my eyes to watch him. Even with the mask, it was obvious he was studying every inch of me. His hands made a quick path down my torso, curling in the edges of my panties. I wondered if he could hear my heart, the blood in my ears was close to deafening.

He's going to see all of me. Will he notice how turned on I am?

I quivered as he began deliberately sliding the garment down. As the panties pulled past my hips, exposing my soft strip of light curls, they stuck to my lower lips from how damp I had become.

Onyx grinned at the vision of my black panties coated in my juices. He tugged them to the floor. "Did you enjoy being punished that much? Were you disobeying on purpose?"

"No," I gasped, covering my mouth. "No, I wasn't, really!"

"Shh," he whispered, wickedly amused. Firmly, he grabbed my thighs. "This is just a sign of your nature, being submissive is something you obviously enjoy. I told you... you're a slave."

He can't be right. I'm not... I was never like this before.

He was so close to my most private of places, I couldn't pretend I didn't want him to explore further.

A gloved finger traced along the edge of my pussy. I groaned, body flooding with anticipation. *Oh god, keep going, please just touch me!*

Onyx placed his thumbs on either side of

my folds, spreading me gently, revealing my slick pinkness. "You're perfect, Opal. A true jewel."

Whimpering, my nails formed half-moons in my palms. Carefully, I eased my fists away, folding my arms over my chest. Hugging myself, I watched Onyx as he knelt at my feet with his smirk so near my clit.

"Please," I blurted, then clasped my lips in shock. He said nothing, only looked at me in silence.

Shit, I made him mad again. I talked without his permission.

I didn't want him to spank me again. Lifting my hands, I bumbled through an apology. "I'm sorry! I didn't mean to speak out!"

Laughing, he let me go and stood straight, peering down at me curiously. "So worked up, aren't you?"

"Yes, Master," I admitted.

"Kneel," he pointed. I didn't hesitate; I dropped down at his feet, a bit smoother than the last time. "This is another lesson for you. The greatest gift a slave can give to her Master, is doing what he desires. Your own pleasure will revolve around that, do you understand?"

No, not really.

Resisting the urge to argue, I bowed my head. "Yes, Master."

"Look at me," he said.

Blinking, I saw that his hand was rubbing along the front of his pants, the shape of his hard-on obvious. My heart skipped a beat. "Take care of this for me," he whispered.

I knew what he expected me to do. It was overwhelming, this primal ache that wanted to free his cock, to see it and taste it...

I was baffled by my visceral reaction.

Never had I been so aroused, I was close to wriggling on the damn floor. Onyx had managed to work me up into a frenzy, his tactics shifting until I was eager to please him.

Licking my lips, I reached up with hands that suddenly seemed very small. Gingerly, I rolled them across the front of his trousers, feeling the firm curve of his manhood pushing against the material eagerly.

Gripping the zipper, I peeled it down. Though I was no virgin, I still gasped when his length bobbed into view. The head of his cock was plump. It was glistening with precome, telegraphing that he was just as excited as I was.

Briefly, I glanced up at him through my eyelashes. Onyx inclined his head, giving me permission.

Wrapping my shaking hand around his base, I marveled at how hot he was. The veins along his shaft flexed under my touch. Aiming the tip at my mouth, I gave an experimental lick.

Onyx groaned deeply, my thighs clenching at the sound. Feeling a unique desire to please this man, I slid my tongue down to his root. I was moving slow, kissing his salty skin.

He didn't want to be teased.

"Take me in your mouth," he demanded, gripping my messy hair. The ornate coif had begun to come loose.

Quickly, I tried to fit him past my wet lips. He was thick, forcing me to adjust fast as he shoved himself down my throat with a grunt. I hadn't given many blow jobs in my life. My dating history was a little sparse—and bland.

With all the time spent on trying to make it into college, I'd had other priorities.

Onyx was insistent, I was thrilling over his desperation. He tasted tangy and sweet, my lips statically charged from the sensation of him sliding in and out.

If he wanted to test my skill, he wasn't letting me show it—but thank god for that. His hand gripped hard on my scalp, using my long tresses for leverage.

Pumping into my face, he fucked my mouth with little care for how I handled it. The wildness, the rough way he moved, it had me burning with desire.

There was a comfort in allowing someone else to be in control. All my life, I'd struggled and fought, taking care of myself and making my own decisions. Onyx had flipped my world, showing me what it was like to be along for the ride.

It was intoxicating.

His shaft swelled in my throat, I knew he was going to finish.

Will he let me pull away? Is he going to...

I understood quickly that he planned to come in my mouth. That fact brought pure ecstasy. He held me still, growling low, raw, as his length began to throb. His seed flowed, thick as syrup, down into my belly.

Working my tongue, I swallowed it all.

Onyx pulled free, and I gasped hoarsely for air. I'd forgotten I needed something as common as oxygen. Wiping my mouth with the back of my wrist, I struggled to gather my thoughts. I was lost, battling my heat, fighting with a side of myself that had seemingly grown over night.

Onyx pet my head softly. "Good, that was lovely."

Staring up at him, my cheeks flared up. Should I feel pleased by his comment or not? I was spared from deciding when he reached into his pants, pulling forth something small.

A pocket watch.

A gorgeous, shockingly familiar pocket watch.

That... no, it can't be!

His frown was brittle, just the sight of him looking unhappy made my stomach twist. "Hmn. It seems we're out of time. We'll have to continue this another time." Turning back, he gazed over my nude form. His lips twisted up on one side. "You *will* come back, my little jewel."

It wasn't a question.

Not for him...

Or for me.

"Yes, Master."

He couldn't have known why I was going pale. Or why the sweat on my spine had become cold.

Onyx tucked that watch away, but I didn't need another look. I knew what it was, and who, exactly, it belonged to. All along, I'd thought I was dealing with two men who had, at most, some odd similarities.

Now I knew the truth.

Seth and Onyx were one and the same.

- Chapter Nine -
Naomi

We returned to the main room together. I'd redressed, looking no worse on the surface.

Inside, I was a turmoil of confused feelings.

There were many people gathered around, casually talking. Some wandered out through the purple curtain. The night was over, the attendants were saying farewells and commenting on the general event as a whole.

One of the men from earlier, I thought his name had been Helm, waved Onyx over. He started to move, then turned back to smile at me. "No doubt he wants to talk about how his own training session went. I'm usually one of the last to leave, don't wait around. I'll see you next time." It was curt, but that suited me just fine.

I know why you'd be last to leave.

"Yes, Master," I whispered, waving slightly. Trying not to appear suspicious, I peered out into the small room. There was nothing but the table and clipboard. *I guess Corbin leaves after everyone signs in.*

On fast feet, I scurried up the stairs, cracking the gold door just enough to view the mansion's entrance room. There was only one person I had to avoid, not two.

I knew where Seth was, after all.

It seemed quiet, so I took the opportunity to slip out and rush up to my guest room. Inside, I almost slammed the door, my lungs deflating.

What happened down there tonight, what was that? Why did I go along with it?

And what do I do, now that I know his secret?

Pulling off the mask, I buried it back in the chest. Peeling the dress away, I hung that up as well, as far back in the closet as I could.

The space was big enough, and full enough, of so many different outfits, I figured no one would even notice it had been worn. I couldn't let anyone see it; they'd recognize it, and my game would end.

This isn't a game.

Walking into the private bathroom in just my lingerie, I caught a glimpse of myself in the full mirror. My ass still displayed the clear hand prints of a certain Dom.

Wincing, I twisted for a better look. *I hope that doesn't bruise.*

Even though I grimaced as I touched the area gingerly, something deep inside of me pulsed with heat. Remembering the spanking,

130

as well as my lack of release through the entire debacle, I brushed my stomach and sighed.

That whole event... it was frustrating, but exciting, too. Will it be like that next time? I caressed my lips, thinking of how his come had tasted. *Oh god, next time.*

Am I actually going to go back?

Even after I know who he is?

I ached to learn what else my 'training' would entail.

Closing my eyes, I imagined how his gloves had felt, how the rope on my wrists had bound me. He'd shown me how good he could make me feel, and even the punishment had been arousing.

Is something wrong with me? What am I thinking? I'm supposed to be here to paint that wall, not involve myself in a secret seedy dungeon.

That thought gave me pause. Why *did* Seth allow this to go on below his mansion?

Why did he partake in it?

It was a side of the man I hadn't expected. But, in hindsight, it was fitting. Seth had told me he enjoyed control. Now, I knew how deep that desire went.

If he finds out that I'm Opal...

I pictured him snapping at me, kicking me out and destroying what I'd worked for. It was possible he'd keep the letter from me. I couldn't blame him—this was a huge betrayal I was committing.

Swallowing nervously, I turned towards the shower to start the water flowing.

He can never find out.

But dammit, if I could only talk to him, I could get all the answers I craved. The knowledge he'd probably fire me right away made me feel sick.

Standing in the hot steam, my wet lashes tickled my cheeks. The watery vibrations felt good, like a massage on my tense skin. When they drummed on my sensitive rear cheeks, I flinched, but held steady. The scalding water was cleansing.

No, I decided, imagining Seth's angry blue eyes. *I already made my decision. I have to stand by it.*

I felt my throat, recalling how Onyx—Seth—had touched me.

He can never know that I went down there.

Or that I'm going to go back.

****

I woke the next day to the sound of my phone going off.

My dreams involving firm hands and whispered words were interrupted. Groaning, I fumbled around until I found the cellphone. Gripping it, I buried my head under the blankets. "Hello?"

"Hey, Naomi?"

The voice was familiar, my brain slowly forming a mental picture. "Veronica, is that you?"

"In fact, it is! Hey, I hadn't heard from you in awhile. Thought I'd just, you know, check in."

I was delighted by the surprise, yet I sensed something in the woman's voice that was frazzled. "It's good to hear from you. Is everything alright?"

"Of course!" Veronica laughed, a hollow sound. "I just had this weird feeling something was up. I don't know, maybe I'm crazy, but I wanted to check in on you to see... well."

To see if I ever got in touch with Seth.

The clarity hit me. "Right. You're curious if I ever took Mr. You-Know-Who up on his offer, aren't you?"

The voice on the line sounded startled, rising in pitch. "What! No, no, why would you ever—okay, you got me." Sighing, Veronica gave a weak giggle. "I mean, what happened at the gallery was just strange. Can you blame me for wanting to get filled in?"

"Not at all." I smiled, a bit flattered to be on the girl's mind. "Look, I'm a little busy, but do you want to get some brunch today?"

"That sounds pretty perfect, want me to come to you?"

I hesitated, thinking about the clearly stated instruction to not invite anyone over without permission.

Do I want to go ahead and just break every rule? I can't bring her here without asking Seth if it's okay.

That might be fine, sort of, except if Veronica came to the mansion, she'd have a million questions. I was a little embarrassed just picturing how she'd look at me, what she would assume once she saw where I was living these days.

Plus, the idea of Seth cornering us and making conversation... how Veronica would inspect our interaction, seeing my flustered mood...

No. No way.

Rocking off of the bed, I flexed my toes. "Let's meet up somewhere else."

****

Dressed in one of the nicer, casual outfits from my temporary closet—a pair of designer jeans and a silk top—I stepped out of the car with Corbin's assistance. As I turned around to look over the small cafe, I saw Veronica gaping at me through the window.

My heels, which I was sure cost more than my monthly rent, clicked across the sidewalk, then the tiled floor of the eatery. I'd tried to find simpler shoes, but Seth didn't really believe in 'simple.'

I hadn't even sat down across from Veronica before she blurted out her first question. "Did you just have someone drive you here? Was that *your* driver? *Do you have a personal driver?*"

Laughing with chagrin, I settled into the booth and wagged my hands. "No, no, relax. He's only taking me places while I'm working for Seth."

Veronica lowered her eyebrows, mouth coiling into an amused smirk. "Oho! So, you did take the job, then."

She's right to the point. "I did, yeah, it was a really good opportunity and..."

Lifting her arms, Veronica spread her fingers. "No need to explain. It has to be pretty good if it came with your own chauffeur. What is he having you paint, a whole collection, just for him?"

"More like a wall in his house."

"You mean his sprawling estate

mansion?"

She'd caught me off guard. Blushing, I spilled some of the water the waiter had just dropped off. Veronica beamed, reminding me of a big cat on a hunt. "How did you know about where he lives?" I asked.

"I don't know *where* he lives, he keeps that pretty secret—though I guess you know, right?" When I nodded quickly, she shrugged. "The power of the internet! I just looked him up in a little research. I knew he was rich, but did you know he's an actual billionaire?"

Wincing, I dabbed at the water stains on my shirt. I'd suspected Seth Hart was overwhelmingly rich, but a billionaire?

What do you even do with that much money?

The memory of the softly lit corridor below his home swam through my mind.

I guess you run a super secret sex club.

The waiter came by once more, and we politely ordered our food. Once we were alone again, I began explaining the situation to Veronica.

She didn't smother her emotions, leaning close as I detailed my past few days. I told her about everything; the first phone call, the admission letter, the gigantic contract, even how Seth had given me free reign to paint whatever I wanted.

136

I kept nothing from her—except the golden door and what lay behind it.

As I finished, Veronica was openly gawking.

"Naomi, this guy... he must *really* like you, huh?"

"Excuse me?" I dropped my straw in my glass, staring. "What the hell do you mean?"

Veronica rolled her eyes, stirring her ice around idly. "Don't tell me you didn't realize. Why else would he offer you all of this?"

"Because he likes my art," I spat, anger coating my tongue.

But, deep down, she'd hit at the root of my worry. From the start, I'd been suspicious of how Seth had handled me. Even if he liked my art, the way he stood close to me... how he seemed to inhale my existence, or stare through my clothes with his piercing eyes...

If Seth liked me, that opened a new issue.

He doesn't know I'm Opal. Why would he flirt with me, as Naomi, while he was content to touch and tease me down in that dungeon?

The heavy knot in my stomach grew by the second. Was Seth that kind of person? Opal or Naomi, was I just some play thing to him?

Veronica broke through my thoughts.

137

"Don't get me wrong, I like your work, too. But someone doesn't just offer you a driver, and lodging, and access to expensive clothing and what have you just so you'll paint a *wall*. Do *you* like *him?*"

"What!" I fixed my wide eyes on the girl across from me. "Do I what? I don't even... I don't know! I hardly know the guy."

Lies. I know more about him than he realizes.

"He's handsome, right?"

"Maybe," I muttered, thinking about when he had shared the pool with me. Beyond that, I couldn't separate him from Onyx. I'd let him touch me.

I'd sucked his damn cock.

Everything about Seth Hart was incredibly attractive. Flushing, hoping Veronica didn't notice, I took a huge gulp of icy water. It did nothing to cool me down.

Veronica waved her straw side to side. "I did mention he's rich, right? What's the problem? Why haven't you locked that down?"

"Veronica!" Scowling, I stared into my glass, cheeks pink as roses. My mind danced with images of Seth; how he would look at me as I worked, the deep sound of his voice.

The firm, strong gloves he'd used on my skin.

That swoon-inducing scent.

Combining my experiences with Seth and Onyx, morphing them into one person, was draining me. "I don't know," I said softly. "I guess I'm not sure he wants me, not like you're saying. What if he's just a playboy? Flirting meaninglessly with me?"

"Well." She shook her head. "I think this guy wants more than your art. And if you *don't* want more from him, you need to be careful. Someone is going to get hurt, and my advice, is don't be around if it's going to be the guy with all the power and money. I'd hate to see what a man like him does when he's rejected."

I gazed at Veronica, trying to find the right words. "I'll admit, I do like him, but..."

But he's kinky.

Frightening.

And he can never know what I know about him.

"He might be more than I can handle," I said carefully.

Canting her head like a bird, the other woman leaned closer over the table. "Don't stop there! What's he done to you? Is he a good kisser? A bad kisser?"

I've only put my lips on his cock.

"We haven't kissed," I said quickly. "No, uh, he's just kind of intense."

"You haven't kissed, but he's too intense?"

"You met him. You have to know what I mean."

"I guess he was a little intimidating," she mused. "But I have a feeling you're not telling me everything."

Kicking my feet under the table, I toyed with a napkin.

Throwing her arms in the air, Veronica sighed. "Give me something to work with!"

I can't tell her what he's done to me.

The memory alone had me rubbing my thighs together. "He's got a nice body," I whispered sheepishly.

She sat back in the booth and waved the waiter over. "I can't really comment on that. You said you saw him when he was swimming, but I'm guessing you haven't seen him naked."

Shame crawled its way to my eyeballs. *No,* I thought, *But he's seen me.*

I opened my mouth warily. "Maybe you're right, and Seth likes me, and I'm being stupid about not jumping on that. It's just, I don't think I'm ready to find out. He's not the only one who would be hurt by rejection."

My friend smiled, reaching across to grab my wrist. "Hey, you don't need to justify it to anyone. It's not my business to tell you what

to do, I'm only teasing—and a little jealous."
She winked. "Besides, you didn't listen to me
about avoiding Seth Hart. Why would you
listen to me about chasing him?"

I smiled shyly, nodding my head to be
polite. Inside my skull, my thoughts were a
hornet's nest. I did like Seth... and Onyx. But
what did I really know about them—him?

*I know he can get me to do things I
never imagined before.*

Knowing Veronica couldn't learn the
truth, I grabbed my drink and didn't bring my
relationship worries up again the rest of our
brunch.

When Corbin pulled up outside, we
hugged each other tightly and promised to get
in touch again soon.

"Maybe I can come visit you and see
your painting?" Veronica asked.

Though I was terrified of introducing
someone else to that mansion with its strange,
dark secrets, I gave a quick nod and ducked
into the car. "Okay, maybe sometime soon!"

We waved through the windows, the
white noise of the engine taking over. When I
was out of eyesight, I stared straight ahead.

She thinks I should get closer to Seth.

Was she right?

I just didn't know anymore.

I'd danced around telling Veronica the real issue—Seth had a double life, and he didn't know that I knew. I was behind the curtain, but Seth, he was juggling what he thought were two different woman.

It was possible that he didn't like me—not the real me.

What will I do if he only wants Opal?

- Chapter Ten -
Naomi

The day stretched by far too slow.

I was lost in a daze, thinking about the other night, and the erotic things I'd partaken in.

The very idea of it, kneeling at someone's feet and calling them 'Master' was so far out of my realm. If I'd been told about it in regards to anybody else, I would have laughed.

Yet, here I was, biding my time until I could rush back through that golden door, folding on the ground in front of Onyx.

Closing my eyes, I breathed in slowly, imagining what he'd done to me.

How he'd teased me, so close to licking my soaked pussy, and instead forcing his hard cock down my throat.

The sound of his voice, that low baritone that penetrated my bones... I wanted to hear him call me his 'little jewel' again.

"Beautiful," that voice whispered.

It was so real, so close to my ear.

Yes, he thought I was beautiful.

Again, it brushed along my neck, stating how I was...

"Beautiful."

I jumped, jerking around to fast I hurt my back. Seth grinned at me, eyes twinkling wickedly. For a split second, my mind went to war. It demanded I kneel, subjugating myself in front of my Master.

No, don't! I locked my knees. *He'll know!*

Grabbing at my chest, I laughed weakly. "You surprised me again!"

"Sorry. Sometimes I walk too softly, it's unconscious." He inclined his head, turning to view the wall I'd been painting. "I was admiring how this is coming along. It's wonderful, it looks like it will be done soon."

I'd been in Seth's home for over a week, now, working away diligently. It amazed me how the the time had flown by.

Brushing my hair behind an ear, I shot him a sideways look. It took great effort to calm my heart. *I was really daydreaming, there. How embarrassing, I hope he didn't notice.* "I think maybe another week or so, yeah."

"That quickly?" He dusted down the front of his crisp jacket. I couldn't help but notice it was a different garment than the one I'd splashed paint on. I didn't have the guts to ask if he'd thrown the other one out.

He's a billionaire, remember? He can afford a hundred new suits when he feels like

144

it.

I wiped my stained hands on my shorts self-consciously. "Yes, if all goes well, I'll be out of your hair by then."

Saying it out loud, regret cut into my chest.

Then I'll have to leave.

I'll never see that dungeon again.

How had I not thought about that until now? Once I was finished with the mural, Seth would have no reason to keep me here. Then... when he expected Opal to show up... and she—I —didn't, how would he feel?

"What if I wanted you to stay longer?"

My reaction was delayed. I almost stepped backward, digesting his words. *Is he serious?* "Why would you want that?" I recalled Veronica's comments about how Seth had a thing for me.

He probably just likes the attention... or... or something.

Dammit, I couldn't make sense of this.

Shrugging, he tucked his hands into his pockets casually. "I have other rooms I'd like painted."

Other rooms? I peeked at the gold door below us, sure that he'd noticed. Seth said nothing about it, only smoothed a hand over his styled hair. "Think about it, you might find

145

staying here longer to be to your benefit."

Excitement welled inside of me.

Oh yes, I knew how I would benefit.

Onyx will have more time with me. The decadent thought had me thrilling. Eyeing the mural, a new thought—an old thought that had gotten buried until now—surfaced.

CCAD will be enrolling again soon. How could I balance painting for Seth, with wanting the letter that would allow me access to the future I'd been chasing?

Swaying on my heels, I said, "I was really hoping to catch the next admission period at CCAD."

"You could do both. Think of the money you'd save staying here, and Corbin could take you to the campus everyday. At night, you could work on your art here. Wouldn't it be perfect?"

I parted my lips, then closed them. *That would be amazing.*

It was also terribly risky.

Here, I'd be able to build up funds, go to class, and achieve my dreams.

I'd also be tempted—constantly—to break the rules as I ran off to meet Onyx. I couldn't hide my identity from Seth forever. Surely, the more time I spent here, the greater the risk?

But...

"I'll consider it, okay." The words escaped. I couldn't get them back.

"Good." He beamed, a smile that was much more genuine and cheerful than any I'd seen him wear before.

"Does that idea make you that happy?" I asked, arching my eyebrows.

Seth's shoulders went stiff. "What do you mean?"

Pointing, my own mouth tugged up at the corners. His mood was contagious. "You just... I've never seen you smile so much before."

As if waking up, his face melted back into the usual relaxed lines. "I guess I *am* in a good mood. But never mind, I've got things to do, so I'll leave you to it." He spun on his polished heels. I could sense the restrained speed in him, he was fighting the urge to jog down the steps.

I watched him go, confused by what had just happened.

Could it be...

No. Was I so egotistical?

But then, why couldn't it be about me?

Even if it *was* about me...

Which ME had him so happy?

He asked me to stay. That can't be

about just my art. Seth was growing fond of me. I wasn't crazy. His smile was too real.

Then again... Thinking about the last encounter with Onyx, I propped my elbows on the railing. *Did I leave a good impression in the dungeon? Is it Opal that's got him so cheerful?*

My hand slipped further up my cheek. Uncertainty roiled through my veins. I couldn't tell what Seth wanted.

Maybe he desires both of us.

My playboy assumption was right. He didn't care if he indulged in two different women. Seth was rich—powerful. He had to be used to getting everything.

I'm not special.

Not at all.

Turning back to the painting, I forced the grim worries away with more work.

****

I was bursting with anxiety, pacing my room and wondering if my plan was actually a good idea.

I hadn't seen anyone go through the golden door in days. Clearly, the events didn't happen every night.

But just minutes ago, people had

knocked—and Corbin had let the masked attendees inside the mansion.

If I go back, what then? It was wild before, even if I came out in one piece, but couldn't it get worse?

I had no idea what Onyx might have planned. The only other thing I'd seen in that dark place was the sexual torture of that blonde girl.

My new Master had exposed my inner desires. It was funny, remembering how I'd struck him, demanding he release me. I'd been angry, rebellious.

He'd proven I didn't really want to leave at all.

Onyx had climbed inside my head. Now, he could command me to bow to his wishes without much trouble.

He managed it with bondage, pleasure...

And a spanking.

Thinking of that, I covered my mouth to muffle a moan. *That was incredible. How could it be bad, going back to him?*

Antsy, like I was an addict who demanded a fix, I finally opened up my closet. The mask was where I'd left it, sitting among the others and watching me with empty eye holes.

I scanned the racks for something else to wear, thinking about how Roseli had shown up in something other than black.

There doesn't seem to be any rule about clothing, I guess people just tend to choose darker stuff. Mulling it over, I grabbed an emerald green dress that hugged my body, tight as the way Onyx had gripped my jaw.

Tying my hair up, I stood back to check my reflection. Twirling, I smiled slyly. I could have been anybody, a woman going to some innocent masquerade—not the filthy one I was ecstatic for.

I wonder if he'll like this outfit.

Wanting to please Onyx had become a steady, but insidious craving. I never even worried this much about what I would wear on a date.

This isn't a date, I reminded myself. For a moment, I looked into the mirror. I couldn't see my eyes behind the mask. I felt... different.

But maybe that was for the best.

Seeking the calmest part of my mind I could dig up, I left the room. Peering down from the railing revealed that the foyer was empty, so I hurried down the stairs.

Gripping the brassy wood, I noticed I was shaking. *Is it from fear, or anticipation?*

Deciding it didn't matter, I'd already come this far, I slipped through and into the dim passage.

At the bottom, I slowed, my blood rushing the closer I got to the purple curtain. Though I was readying myself for it, I nearly bolted when I saw Corbin.

There wasn't a line like last night; one or two people were finishing up, exiting through the drapes as I approached. The chauffeur glanced up at me, his face neutral and impossible to read.

Does he know, did he figure it out somehow? No, calm down!

Gripping the pen on the clipboard, I paid attention this time to the page I was signing. I didn't need to repeat the surprise of last night's role call.

With one more covert look at Corbin, I walked through the curtain and into the strange, underground world hidden beneath the Hollywood mansion.

The room was emptier than last night. *They were all here to watch the new slaves get called. Now...*

Now, I realized, the other members were off enjoying themselves elsewhere in the tunnels. Turning in place, I nearly slammed right into Onyx before I had a moment to wonder where he might be.

The noise I made was a small, squeaky breath of air. He seemed as much a part of this place as the gold door itself.

His outfit was tight, charcoal. The shirt was open, displaying his glistening rows of ivory muscles.

Still, always with those gloves.

Hugging his long fingers, the smooth material caught the light, displaying the texture for a moment. Onyx linked his hands behind his back, wordlessly staring down at me with an aura of pure confidence.

It filled me, made my knees weak and my tongue swollen.

Kneel, kneel, I reminded myself as I fought the distracting fog in my brain.

Carefully, trying to be more elegant than last time, I dropped to the floor and bowed my head. With my legs bare as they were, I was grateful for the plush rug.

"Hello, little jewel," he mumbled, sounding like he was more pleased than he wanted to admit. Something touched the top of my head, tracing down to brush my temple. It was clearly his hand. When he tilted my face up, he smiled. "Did you miss me?"

"Yes, Master," I whispered, knowing it was true.

His laugh was rich and dark as molasses. "Follow me." He let me go, turning to walk away. Where he had touched me, my skin was scalding with anticipation.

Standing quickly, I followed behind him down the tunnel.

I watched how he moved, enjoying the gentle sway of his wide shoulders. He had a powerful grace, like a hunting panther.

Not paying attention to where we were going, I almost didn't recognize that I'd been down this passage before. When we passed through the open curtains, and I saw the familiar couches, that unforgettable table, I knew.

This is the room I wandered into the first night!

The room where I'd watched the blonde woman get fucked.

Inside, there were no other people, but my nerves still sparked as I stared around. *Why did he bring me here?*

"Come." He'd moved to stand by that foreboding table, his tone revealing he couldn't even conceive of me resisting. On legs as unstable as wet spaghetti, I walked towards him.

Mere feet away, we sized each other up. I was trying to judge his face, the cut of his smile, looking for any sign that could help me predict what was about to happen.

For his part, Onyx only parted his lips in a toothy grin. "You look lovely tonight. It's a shame you won't be wearing that dress for

153

long."

Those words, mentioned so calmly and factually, caused me to swoon. My mouth went dry, keeping me from speaking. I was grateful for that. *Arguing with him would only make this worse.*

"Take it off, girl." He flicked a finger at me, strict as ever.

If I don't listen, will he spank me again?

The concept filled me with a burning lust, quick as lightning. Excited by his firm instructions, the way he stood there, unwavering in his position of power, I forced my hands to the hem of my dress.

Inching it up, I pulled it over my head, like tearing off a bandage. If I gave myself too much time to ponder my actions, I was worried I'd freak out. My mask, caught in the motion, almost pulled free. *Shit!*

The last thing I needed right then was for Onyx to recognize me.

Flustered, I adjusted it and let the green garment fall to the floor. Standing there in my lingerie, I fidgeted, tempted to cover myself.

My master nodded his head, silently approving. "Now the rest."

Of course, did I expect any less?

Reaching back, I unclasped the bra, shooting a look at the entrance as I did so. Still, no one entered, and I calmed at the idea we would remain alone. Hooking into the elastic of my panties, I slid them down my thighs. They joined the collection at my feet.

In only my simple flats, I waited patiently for Onyx to instruct me again.

"Good girl. Lay across the table on your stomach and grab the ledge."

My intuition had expected this, but I still coiled and twisted like I'd eaten live snakes. *It's going to happen, I'm going to end up like that blonde woman.*

It struck me, then, how odd it was to not even know that girl's name.

Stepping forward, I leaned over the long table, the surface cool under me. It pressed on my hipbones, my body stretching as far as it could to hold the far edge. The temperature made me shiver, my nipples hardening where they were crushed beneath.

Lifting my head, I glanced back to see Onyx standing behind me, openly admiring the view. With my feet slightly apart, I knew nothing was left to his imagination.

Blushing furiously, I started to bring my legs together to keep some of my dignity.

"No," he snapped, freezing me. "Spread your legs, wide as you can, and don't you dare try to move them."

This is humiliating, I thought silently.

Despite that fact, my core was throbbing with sudden lust.

Knowing he had his eyes fixed on me, I slid my heels to the sides. I was sure it was far enough, but Onyx kicked them out even wider. My quads strained, trembling in their extreme position.

I don't know if I can hold this.

Firm, familiar, his gloves gripped my ankles, shackling them into place. I whimpered, understanding how vulnerable I truly was.

I could hardly see him from my angle.

But I could feel him.

Languidly, Onyx ran his palms up my calves, on and on until he tickled the back of my taut hamstrings. His voice rang with the smirk I couldn't see. "Your scent is amazing."

A rush of desire took hold, I bit my tongue to try and smother it.

Onyx rose up, standing between my wide thighs, his hands resting on my hips. It was lewd. If he wanted to, he could pull his cock free and slide it inside without any input from me.

Why is that so hot? I don't understand anything anymore!

I should have been more scared, but my attention was focused acutely on the feel of his gloves. He rolled them up, grazing lightly across the top of my ass. "Your bruises have healed, I hope the memory of them helps you behave today."

"Y—yes, Master," I breathed out, wishing he would touch me a bit lower. My pussy twitched, wanting attention, but he didn't offer it.

"Tonight," he said, "I'm going to teach you a lesson in patience, as well as worth. I want you to understand what it means to belong to someone."

My eyes bulged behind the mask. He was digging deep, packing erotic ideas into my skull. Fear wasn't enough to keep my pussy from turning into a furnace.

"I'm going to put a show on for everyone, and you'll be the star." He squeezed my ass cheeks until I grimaced. "You'll learn I can do *whatever I want* to you, Opal. Doesn't that sound good?"

Did it sound *good?*

How could I respond to that? I was burning up from my toes to my throat, skin already shiny from exertion. This man I'd given myself to, a the man I'd shared wine with as we toured his home, was tormenting me.

That was enough, but to do so with an audience?

My answer wavered as it rose in my

157

throat. "Yes, Master."

What is he going to do to me?

Onyx smiled, a look that curled through my lower belly and squeezed. Moving away, he wandered over to a small desk. As he rustled in it, I heard the first foot steps. *Oh, god, no!*

They entered quietly, but not because they needed to. The men waved to Onyx, who nodded his head as they settled in. There were some women with them, all wearing various collars around their throats.

All of Onyx's talk about slaves had opened my awareness to the metal and leather accessories.

The only girl without a collar lifted her head, long enough to meet my eyes. Startled, I recognized her. *One of the other new submissives, I think her name was Tara?*

Toying with her curly brown hair, she looked away quickly, as if ashamed to be witnessing me on the table. *Will she go through this, too? Why is Onyx doing this to me, first?*

Confused by the situation, I placed my forehead on the flat surface. If I could have stayed like that, pretending I was alone, I would have.

Something firm brushed my lower back; I gasped and let go of the table.

Instantly, Onyx spanked me, his voice

barking. "Did I tell you to let go of the ledge?"

"No, sorry Master!" I grabbed hold again, praying he'd be satisfied.

Placing whatever he had touched me with on my spine, as if I, myself, were a table, he moved in front of me. Grabbing my hands, he forced my wrists into a pair of padded cuffs. The shackles clicked into place, unyielding.

I was trapped.

He breathed out, and I looked up. Our noses were inches away, his lips cruel with their nearness. Through the shade of his mask, I saw the cobalt centers of those gorgeous eyes. He was as good as a god of the ocean, I could have swam in his vision and lost myself.

It was magnetic.

It was illogical.

Onyx was displaying me to a full room and I still hadn't even *kissed* the man.

He could kiss me now, I thought, fixated on his ruddy lips. They were plush looking, a mouth that I had seen form smirks, and smiles... and frowns.

I was positive, if he kissed me, it would throttle my senses until my brain fried into useless charcoal. Nothing could feel so good as his lips.

It would be the epitome of pleasure.

Kiss me, I willed him.

159

His eyes smoldered. Then he was gone, removing the weight from my spine and heading behind me.

Cold sadness infected me. I looked over my shoulder, nervous about what he had planned.

Onyx held something in his glove, it was silvery and attached to a bundle of cloth. He didn't seem intent on explaining; he lowered it towards my thighs, wordlessly pressing it against my pussy.

My senses demanded I bolt, but I couldn't move away. With my muscles tight and my belly quaking, he hooked the straps around my hips. He fastened them, something pressing firmly on my slit and along the crease of my ass.

"There," he purred, stroking all the way up to the base of my neck. "Little jewel, what I have planned should be very... fun." He waved outward, indicating the people reclining on the sofas, girls kneeling by their feet. "I'm going to turn on this toy, and then we're all going to watch you come over, and over, and over."

Darkness crept through his liquid smile.

"Until I decide you're done," he added flatly.

I couldn't stop myself from crying out. "No!" My body glowed from a full-figure blush. "You can't do that to me!"

Onyx scowled, slapping the outside of my thigh. "I thought you'd learned not to speak out."

"Master, please, I..."

I can't do this! It's too much, no!

Not long ago, I'd struggled with being nude in privacy with this man. How could he expect me to endure the humiliation of public orgasms?

"I'm not an exhibitionist," I insisted desperately.

"You're whatever I want you to be." In disbelief, I watched him go, his back to me as he approached the group. The room was small, the gathering only a few yards away from my obscene display. Lowering his head, he spoke softly to someone, leaving me in frantic anticipation.

Did he decide not to turn this thing on? Is it broken, maybe, and he doesn't know?

Onyx gazed my way with a sideways smile. Then I saw it; in his hand, lifted at eye level, was a tiny remote. If I hadn't been looking, I wouldn't have seen his thumb press the button.

It wouldn't have mattered. I felt the result soon enough.

The vibrations poured through my hips, waking my clit up in a roar of sensation. Any hope I had of keeping myself quiet vanished as

161

the device's electric waves grew higher.

I thrummed, a live wire, my breathing coming in hard and fast gasps.

No, not this... I can't take this!

It was too powerful. It almost hurt.

Good, let it! I grasped at the discomfort, trying to make it my armor. I only had so much dignity, I refused to lose it all be coming in front of all these strangers.

My skin was sweating profusely. Helplessly, ignoring how I worked to clench my jaw, my lips parted in wanton passion. *No, please! I shouldn't enjoy this!*

Everyone was watching me... and I couldn't control myself. Couldn't bury the delicious, slow burn of arousal as it crawled from my thighs to the deepest part of me. My insides squeezed, wanting to be filled.

Wrapped in a world of forced pleasure, I began to buckle.

I'm really going to do it—oh my god, I'm going to come!

I squeezed everything, pulled at my bonds, but there was no escape. Not from the table, not from the eyes, and certainly not from the device driving me to orgasm.

Onyx wanted to show me his power. He could bend me to his will and make me do things I'd never normally allow.

This man... how can he...

I couldn't focus, my eyes crinkling shut. Color bloomed, a fireworks show behind my lids. I groaned obscenely, remembering how the blonde woman had done the same. The pressure was building, my core a bundle of nerves, my pussy soaked and hot.

Closer to the edge I slipped, the vibrations unrelenting.

The toy was snuggling my clit, the strap that threaded through my ass tickling a part of me no one had ever played with. This was beyond erotic, there was no word for this shameful, ever present bliss.

Finally, I crashed helplessly over the cliff, my climax eliciting a squeal. I wished I could bite my tongue, or that Onyx had gagged me again. My body was my enemy, it listened to only one person right then.

Not me.

The man who I called my Master.

Shivering, the last of the orgasm washed down to my cramping toes. I'd have curled them, if they weren't pressed so hard into my shoes.

Somewhere, beyond the blood pounding in my ears, I thought I heard someone chuckling. Lifting my head, I looked back through bleary eyes and saw Onyx smiling at me. He was reclining on a sofa, sipping from a glass and appearing more relaxed than ever.

He lifted a hand, as if in a salute, and squeezed the remote again.

On cue, the device between my legs buzzed more violently, my swelling clit getting no relief. Moaning, I arched my back, shaking my head. *This is too much, I can't, not again!*

My body didn't agree, it pushed along with my heightened senses. My searing skin and fluttering heart made the next orgasm roll through even easier. There was no time to prepare, I was shaking before it hit, and long after it vanished.

Am I really doing this? Am I coming so easily?

The pleasure was transforming into torture. My slick tunnel wanted to be filled. I was deliriously empty, my pussy rippling with its need to be stuffed.

I was growing hazy, the stream of orgasms leaving me weak. At some point I began drooling, whimpering between screams.

Again, Onyx made me come. And again, he simply watched me with his hungry eyes.

My form gyrated what little it could as I moaned. When the vibrations still insisted I sustain the deep soreness, I was sure I'd go insane if I didn't black out first.

Abruptly, the device shut off, my flesh shivering with phantom buzzing. Juices pooled lewdly down my legs and to the floor.

Something touched my thigh, cool in comparison to my hot skin. It moved, trailing down my ass, making me understand it was a hand.

A glove, that's Onyx.

My suspicion was confirmed when he leaned over, breathing in my ear. "Have you had enough?"

My vision swung; I could barely see him. "Yes, Master, I... please, I can't handle..."

"You could, if I wanted you to, correct?"

His curt question shut me up. More of this would ruin me. Fuck, I'd start babbling, I'd have to be carried out.

No, I thought desperately, *I couldn't handle more, even if he wanted me to.*

Onyx stared me straight in the eyes.

And I whispered, "Yes. For you, Master, I could."

It seemed to please him, the straps around my thighs vanishing as he removed the toy.

The air felt good on my wetness, but his fingers, gentle and probing, felt even better. Excitement thickened within me at his exploration. "You're soaked, little jewel, are you sure you're done? Or do you want something else?"

I understood his mind games. Every time I admitted to his questions, a part of me broke down. It made pushing me easier and easier. He was turning me into his slave, just like he said he would.

But I didn't care.

"I... something else, Master." I knew other people would hear me, but I'd been craving this since the beginning. How he'd spoken to me, tempted me to sign up as a submissive...

Wait, I thought, my mind clearing. *No. It was before then.*

I'd hoped for more from Onyx—from Seth—since the day I'd entered his home. Even before I knew this side of him, I'd wanted the handsome, confident man to show me what he could do.

I'd have let him kiss me in his pool, I think, if he'd tried.

I want it, I really do, please...

"Tell me what you need." Spreading my ass cheeks, he traced the slickness that had coated everything.

Internally, I battled with saying it so bluntly. But the pressure inside of me was tight, aching for him to finally fuck me. I'd tasted his cock, where was the harm in giving in and saying that I...

That I need it? Is that it?

"Answer me, girl," he growled, digging his fingers deeper into my backside. I whimpered, especially when the pain only made me yearn for more.

"I want... I want you, Master."

"Cock," he laughed, spanking me lightly. "Say cock. You want my cock."

Blushing furiously, I shut my eyes. "Your cock, I want your cock!" I was amazed at how just uttering that phrase made my clit swell.

Onyx peeled me open, sliding his thumbs along my pinkness. Inhaling sharply, I tried to encourage him to go further, but I could only wiggle so much.

"Tell me more," he breathed, wicked and sensual. "You know what I need to hear. Tell the whole room."

My mind bristled with the memory of that night; the woman tied down like I was now, whimpering at the gold-masked man's touch, his every movement.

He wants me to beg.

So I opened my mouth.

"Please, Master, I need it! I... I need you to fuck me, I'll do anything!"

Onyx chuckled, a harsh sound that only hinted at his own throaty lust. Did he want me as much as I wanted him?

He brought his teeth to my ear and gave

a sharp nibble. It made me moan, but not because it hurt.

"I always knew you'd do anything to have my thick cock spreading you open."

Something about how he said that tugged at the warning center of my brain. I was too mushed up to think deeper.

I didn't hear him free his erection from his pants. I was only aware of that warm head, sliding up and down my soaked folds, teasing me with its presence.

Shuddering, I groaned as he began to push inside of me. His length penetrated slowly, a fact I was both thankful for, and frustrated by.

I wanted more, and didn't want to wait.

Onyx had been trying to teach me patience. I had very little, right then. If I hadn't been tied down, I would have thrust myself back onto him. Instead I tossed my head, clenching him hungrily as he sank further into my pussy.

His shaft spread me completely, stretching me beyond what I thought I could take. But he kept on, his thickness helped by my multiple orgasms. My slickness eased his path.

Onyx grunted with the final inch, my walls hugging him, craving more. Carefully, he began stroking into me, his gloves holding my hips in a vice. His pace was rhythmic; taunting me with his ability to control himself.

How can he be so calm? I'm going insane!

Again, he pumped into me. Again, I cried out in carnal bliss.

I turned my head to watch him. His mouth was slightly parted, teeth bared—a man far more wrapped in his lust than he wanted to show.

He frowned harshly. "Look away, girl."

Disappointed, I put my cheek to the table.

My pouting was brief. His next stroke slammed into my eager pussy. "Aah," I gasped, amazed by how wonderful he felt. Expertly, he reached below, the smooth texture of his glove stroking my needy clit. Perfect little circles, the man knew my body intimately.

He's going to do it, he's going to make me come again!

Nothing could beat the sensation of being stretched around his hard cock. It was constant, never relenting in how it stuffed me.

So worked up, so ready to finally be in the moment, I tensed all over as the waves began. My muscles strangled his cock as it stirred up my insides.

Then he was there, instructing me from

mere inches away, his nose tickling my temple.

"Come for me, Opal, show me how well you can obey."

Like I was a song he knew by heart, an instrument far too familiar in his acute hands, I felt him calling my orgasm to a crescendo. Numb to my own screams, I shook on his cock as his hard chest pressed into my back. So lost in the pleasure, I was dimly aware of his prick when it started to swell.

He's going to finish in me!

I wasn't on birth control. How could I be so reckless?

In a panic, I opened my mouth to argue, but only a hoarse sob escaped.

At the last second, his cock pulled free, the warm spurts of his semen landing on my skin. Breathing heavy, I relaxed on the table while the last of the aftershocks fled my pussy.

I can't believe it, did I really... did he...

I heard someone speaking, was sure it was Onyx. Dampness touched me, rough and sliding over my back. Looking up, I was dismayed when it wasn't my Master, but a girl with long, raven hair.

I've seen her before... what was her name? Cora? She cleaned off the blonde, too, that night.

My ankles were freed, as well as my

wrists, but I didn't move. Everything ached, I was exhausted and wanted to rest. People were talking around me, I caught snippets of conversations.

"...be wonderful, really..."

"...yes, I'm excited for the auction..."

"...think he'll go for her..."

"...oh, he never buys any of them..."

Gingerly, I pushed myself up, weak and unable to stand without the aid of the table. Holding the edge, I turned around, fighting through a cloud of cotton as I regained my composure. *What is everyone talking about, the auction?*

"Here," Cora whispered. The dark haired girl offered me the green dress and lingerie I'd been wearing. Taking it, I redressed quickly, conscious now of my nudity. Once more thankful for the masks we all wore, I tied the gown into place. "Where did Onyx go?"

"*Master* Onyx," she corrected, "Is talking to potential buyers."

"Buyers?"

"Yes." Cora nodded, her collar glinting in the light of a nearby lamp. "All the new submissives are sold off to potential Masters at the auction. The next is two nights from now, Master Onyx plans to put you up."

"What?" Blinking, I stumbled

backwards. "But I... I thought he was, you know, *my* Master?"

Why would he auction me off?

Panic bloomed like a thorny rose inside of me.

The other woman gave an indulgent smile. "No, Master Onyx likes to train the girls, but he never takes any as his own. Someone else will buy you, but don't worry, all the Masters are very excited about you."

I hardly heard her, I was looking around for Onyx. *No, there's no way I'd go with someone else. It's him... him that I...*

Halting my thoughts, scared where they might go, I hurried through the crowd.

Brushing past everyone, each person becoming just a blur, I moved down the tunnel and into the main room. Whipping my head side to side, I finally spotted him. He was standing by the man I recognized as Helm, wrapped in conversation.

I didn't know what I had planned, only that I was suddenly in front of Onyx. My hands were clenched at my sides. I knew my eyes burned with the hurt that rolled in my guts.

Onyx and Helm both paused, staring at me with dubious frowns.

I spoke first.

"You can't auction me off!" Lifting an

172

arm, I cut through the air for emphasis. "Not after everything! I won't let you do that to me! Don't you know that I--"

At once, several things happened.

Helm moved his arm, and I knew he was about to hit me.

Onyx grabbed me by the hair first, forcing me away from the attack and into the ground instead. Yelping from the sharp pain in my scalp, I realized through my shock that cheek was being shoved into the rug.

On my knees, I clawed desperately for the arm holding me still.

Onyx was stronger.

His other hand grabbed my wrists, holding them still, leaving me helpless in his captivity.

"Let me go!" I hissed. I was on the verge of hysteria. Between what my body and mind had endured just minutes ago, and the news from Cora, I was ready to strike.

To fight.

His voice was hot on my temple. The tone he used was frightening; placid, emotionless. "Did you honestly, *honestly*, just walk up and and tell me what I couldn't do, little jewel?"

I opened my mouth to argue, but he squeezed my hair, making me scream briefly instead. When I quieted, hyperventilating into the rug, he pressed on. "It seems I was mistaken, thinking you were ready to be a slave. I don't enjoy being embarrassed like this. I have rules, and they are to be taken seriously. *Always.*"

Rules, I thought bitterly. *I know all about your rules.*

"I'll need to put you through more training instead of auctioning you off, which will disappoint many of the other Doms here. Do you know how that makes me look?" Onyx lifted my head, turning me so our noses touched. Through the holes in his mask, I got a good look at his eyes.

They were boiling with anger, bright and alive with a sense of indignation. They terrified me with how piercing they were, how perfectly blue. I'd seen Seth angry before, but it paled beside this moment.

He pushed me down roughly. "You're lucky the evening is over. Next time, we'll take your training to a new level, rub out this *ridiculous* defiance you have. Go, leave me."

Pressing my forehead to the floor, I stared at the rug blankly.

How could he do this to me?

On weak legs, I knelt, looking up at Onyx and his turned back. Unsure of what else to do, I scrambled, falling through the purple curtains. I fell up the stairs, my eyes blurry with tears I didn't understand.

I was angry—I was furious!

I was also hurt beyond words.

On wobbling legs, I climbed to my room, collapsing on my bed in a heap.

How could Onyx do everything he had to me—with me—and then casually auction me off to another man? Had I meant nothing?

I'm such an idiot.

Those blue eyes smoldered in my brain, reminding me of what I would have to face soon enough. Even if I didn't return to the dungeon below, if I only stayed to finish the painting, I would still have to see him.

To listen to his words, to see the hands that had teased me to orgasm.

Seth... Onyx... they were the same person. I couldn't have one without the other.

Now, cut to my core with the knowledge he didn't even want *me*...

I was lost.

- Chapter Eleven -
Naomi

The shower scalded my skin, but still, it wasn't enough.

I hung my head, hair streaming down, watching the water run down the drain.

It'd be nice if my memories, and my worries, could just go down there too, I thought. Leaning on the tile, I closed my eyelids and tried to get a grasp on my mind.

After last night, everything had been ruined. My head ached with the image of those cold eyes; clear as diamonds, just as unbreakable.

Why. Why did I have to fall for him?

As much as I had questioned my decision to allow my secret lover to get as close as he had, when threatened by being denied more of him, I'd lost it.

I touched my neck, thinking of how he had thrown me down when I'd confronted him.

The auction. How dumb, how ridiculous!

Yet, it bothered me like nothing else.

Imagining being sold to some other faceless Dom was a nightmare.

After all the things he showed me... my biggest fear is losing him.

Does he really never claim subs of his own? If what Cora said was to be believed, then...

Frowning, I brushed a damp strand of hair behind my ear, ignoring it as the shower moved it back out of place. *I lost my mind, for a moment. Told him he couldn't sell me to someone else.* That memory was horrible.

But that wasn't what haunted me now.

I was scared of the auction. But honestly, I've lost him anyway.

I'd been stupid, trying to play this secret game. Staying here to paint more art had been tempting, it would have allowed me to indulge with Seth without ever revealing I knew the truth.

Now, knowing his plans for me, I couldn't keep playing.

I couldn't keep him for myself.

And if I told him what I knew... there was a big chance I'd *still* lose everything.

I can't win.

Gritting my teeth in frustration, I slammed my fist onto the tile wall, over and over until my knees buckled. Crumbling to the bottom of the shower, I hugged myself and sobbed.

I couldn't go back, not after learning I would be sold to someone else. Why would I risk getting caught anymore?

Seth was a cold, strict man. I had no illusion he'd punish once he learned I'd broken his rules. I didn't know how he'd punish me, but Veronica's warning came to mind.

She was scared of what he'd do if I rejected him.

If only she knew my reality.

That damn gold door. I should have just listened to his rules from the start.

But if I had, would I have gotten so close to the man?

You aren't close, I berated myself. *You've been lusting after an illusion.*

It's all a game.

My skin was like a prune when I finally left the bathroom. Wrapped in a robe, I settled on the bed in the guest room. *I just need to finish the mural for him. Once I do that, I'll...*

I'll just leave.

I can't do this anymore. If I go back into that dungeon, I'm just playing with fire.

Thinking of how his smooth gloves had felt on my flesh, his words whispering wickedly in my ear as he made my body tremble with a lust I never knew, I hugged myself.

Right. If I go back, I'll only get hurt.

It's done, it has to be.

Wiping my cheeks, erasing the dampness from my milky skin, I pretended it was water from the shower.

****

The kitchen downstairs was quiet, morning light frail and white where it poured in through all the windows. I moved around on soft feet, the vibe in the air one of respectful solitude.

I wonder where Seth is, or Corbin?

Frowning, I poured myself a glass of milk from the fridge, sipping it as I stood by the backdoor. Outside, the world was green with life.

I wonder if this will be my last week here. If I finish the mural, I'll let Seth know I can't make the time for more projects. That I need to focus on school.

Sighing, I swirled my drink and mumbled softly to myself. "It's for the best, isn't it?"

"Is what for the best?"

The voice came from behind me, close enough that his question moved a strand of my hair. I spun, dropping the glass onto the tiled floor. Together, Seth and I watched the shards

179

of crystal explode, the milk cascading around in a white torrent.

My mouth hung open, eyes frightened as they focused on the equally stunned face of my employer. Seth had his hands lifted, fingers spread like he was trying to protect himself from an oncoming attack.

But I could only stare into his sparkling blue eyes, forced to recall the moment I'd seen them last.

My mind blurred with the memory of his hand in my hair, cheek rubbing into the rug while his words seared through me like red embers.

Oh god, say something, do something!

I quickly moved across the kitchen, grabbing a towel and bending to wipe the spill. "Oh god, I'm so sorry, I didn't mean to—"

"Careful!" he hissed, reaching out in my direction.

I didn't listen, focusing on the wet mess as I soaked it up, my hands rubbing across the tiles. It was then, as I adjusted myself, that my bare foot found the inevitable shard of glass.

"Ah!" I dropped the damp towel, wincing at the surprising pain.

"I warned you!" Seth snapped. Before I could respond, or even try to argue with him, he wrapped his arms around me and scooped me up.

180

Holding me close, he looked at the glittering minefield of glass that was once a safe kitchen floor. "Don't you know better than to move around without shoes on after breaking something?"

My words circled in my throat. He was cradling me protectively, a concept I'd never entertained as a possibility. So far Seth had brought me torture, and he'd gifted me with immense pleasure.

This was something... new.

The slight stubble on his jaw, something usually invisible, stood out. He hadn't even shaved yet. I was close enough to nuzzle him.

Oh shit, what am I thinking!

"Corbin! Corbin, get in here!" Shouting, he turned and carried me into the living room, holding me like I weighed nothing. Pressed against his chest, I inhaled his scent, the heavy olive oil smell I'd noticed on my first night with Onyx.

His eyes fixed on me, searching my face. Gingerly, he set me on one of the couches, kneeling on the rug. "Let me see," he said softly.

"I—what?"

"Your foot, let me see where you stepped on the glass." He gestured impatiently, looking over his shoulder for Corbin.

With his lips not so temptingly close, I

181

was able to clear away my sluggishness. I lifted one leg from where it poked from my bathrobe, regretting my decision to not get changed after my shower.

Seth turned back around, his fingers encircling my ankle. When he leaned in, his nostrils flaring, we both felt my tiny hairs stand straight.

Is he remembering how he tied my legs apart, how he fucked me blind?

"Mr. Hart, what happened?" Corbin had appeared, standing by the hallway and looking concerned.

"Grab me the first aid kit," Seth said. "Ms. Starling stepped on some glass."

"Oh dear, I saw the mess in the kitchen. I'll hurry, one moment." He was gone like a ghost.

Seth looked up at me, brows low, his tone heavy. "Does it hurt?"

"No, not much. It's really not a big deal," I said, forcing a smile.

He clearly didn't believe me. His eyes squinted at my heel, hand he ran a thumb across the bottom. The sharp twang made me jump. He'd brushed the cut, and I openly hissed through clenched teeth. "Alright, yeah," I said. "That hurt."

Corbin crossed the rug on fast feet, kneeling beside Seth, first aid kit in hand. As he pulled out a small bottle and tweezers, it was clear that he was planning on removing the glass himself.

Seth had other ideas.

Without even looking, he reached out and took the items, still peering at my foot. "Thank you, Corbin. That will be all."

I watched the calm, emotionless way the chauffeur remained crouched. Finally, he straightened and gave a slight nod. His eyes were curious when he glanced at me. I shifted with discomfort.

What was that look for?

"As you wish," The driver said, exiting on his perfectly shined shoes towards the kitchen.

The man at my feet touched the tweezers to the wound. Helplessly, I twitched away. "Sorry, I'll try to keep still." I blushed, seeing his frown.

"You don't have much pain tolerance, do you?" he murmured, gripping my ankle as he gently prodded at the small cut. He was very focused, I was caught up in how precisely he worked.

"No," I chuckled. "Not really. I guess you'd have to practice to get used to it, and who would do that?"

"Sometimes an ability to endure pain has its place."

I locked my jaw to keep from commenting.

It was impossible not to recall the spanking he'd put me through on my first night of training. *This is too weird, he doesn't know that I get what he means. Right?*

He thinks he's playing with a hidden deck, but I know all of his cards.

"There," he said, lifting the tweezers with the shard of glass held between them. Wrapping it in a napkin, he set it aside. Holding a bottle, he poured the liquid onto a cotton ball, the scent in the air acrid.

"Peroxide," I groaned, even before he pressed the wet, burning blob to my foot. "Dammit, that stings!"

Seth chuckled, winding a small amount of gauze around my heel and ankle. "Don't complain so much. You're fine now, it was a small thing."

I know, so why did you react like you did?

He'd carried me out of the kitchen like the place had been on fire. Seeing such concern and tenderness from Seth was baffling.

But I...

I liked this side of him.

Frowning, I set my foot on the floor, testing my weight. "Thanks, and sorry about your glass."

"It's fine. I didn't mean to scare you this morning. I was surprised to see you up so early. Did you have some plans?"

Opening my mouth, I hesitated. "Yes. I was going to work on the mural so I can finish it before next week."

He kept his face neutral, but nodded quickly. "I see. Have you given any thought to my offer, then?"

I can't, I just can't stay.

"I... think it would be better if I just got ready to focus on college, my classes. If that makes sense."

Seth was a wall; I couldn't read him. His lips—lips I still itched to kiss even now—were as neutral as the color grey. The only thing that gave me a hint he was upset, was the extra second of silence that slid between us.

Standing, he offered me a hand, his expression stoic. "Ms. Starling, I have nothing but respect for your pursuit of knowledge. I hope you'll decide to come back in the future, when you have the time."

Is he upset? If he is, just wait until Opal never returns.

Warily, I slid my palm in his, noticing how small it felt in his grasp. He helped me up, and I took a careful step. It stung, but it didn't hamper my movement.

"If you'll excuse me, I have some things to attend to. I have an important event in a few days that I need to prepare for." His smile was tight as a drum, his back facing me far too quickly.

I stood there, watching him vanish down the hall. As he left, I turned my head, catching a glimpse of that cursed golden door.

Its surface was shining, mocking me.

Yes, I thought sadly, *I know exactly what event you're planning for, Master Onyx.*

- Chapter Twelve -
Naomi

With long, labored strokes, I painted the mural.

It was the first time I could remember not enjoying my art. For days it had held no joy, no satisfaction. Knowing the piece would be completed soon felt like a guillotine above my head.

Filling my lungs, I pushed air between my tight lips.

This sucks.

There was no better way to frame it. The situation was unfair, I'd been forced to walk away from the thing I wanted most. The thing I hadn't even *thought* I could want.

Dragging the brush over the wall, I saw I'd run out of paint. Scowling, I pulled out my phone to look at the time. *Almost eight. Dammit.* I'd wanted to be done, gone out the door before anyone arrived for this evening's event.

Guess I messed that up, too.

Rubbing my neck, I massaged my knotted muscles. I ached all over, mostly from how awful my sleep had been. *All those nightmares.*

I couldn't stop thinking about his angry eyes, and in my dreams, he would shackle me to a wall, walking away without once looking back.

Abruptly my phone came to life, I almost dropped it in my surprise. Eyeing the number, I brightened up and answered it. "Hey Veronica, what's up?"

"Naomi! Hey! Just calling to check in, see how things were progressing."

"Well," I sighed, facing the painting. "The mural is pretty close to done and—"

"No, silly." Veronica's voice dropped an octave, burning with humor. "I meant the progress with you and Seth."

Tightening my fingers on the phone, I scanned the foyer below. No one had entered the house yet for the auction, but I still felt this conversation was better in private. Scurrying over the floor, I slammed the door of the guest room behind me. "Right. That whole thing."

"'That whole thing.' What a way to phrase it!"

"Veronica, listen. The stuff between me and Seth?" Sliding down the door, I sat on the ground. "It isn't going so well."

The girl on the line made a sympathetic sound. "Do tell."

"It just isn't going to work out. I—I guess you could say I messed up, thought he was

188

someone else."

For a long minute, the willowy woman was quiet. When Veronica spoke next, she was dubious. "Okay, so is the person he *really* is someone bad, someone you don't like?"

Looking down at my feet, at the bandage, I wiggled my toes. "No, he isn't bad. He's just more than I bargained for, maybe? I don't even know. Veronica, there's more to him than I initially suspected."

Her hard laughter wasn't unkind. "Who the hell doesn't have more to them than we think at first? Naomi, you're looking at this all wrong."

"I am?"

"Yes! So your crush has more to him than on the surface. If it's good stuff, what's the big deal?"

What's the big deal?

The big deal was that Seth had a secret life, one I could never be a part of—because he would never let me. At least now I understood why a rich, dashing man like him was single.

The sinister side of him, the person who wanted to claim and dominate, didn't belong in his everyday life.

But then, he apparently doesn't want to keep anyone in his Dom life, either.

What the hell *did* he want?

189

A man who hides from everyone...

My attention roamed over to the closet. "I think," I said softly, "He might be ashamed of a big part of himself."

Veronica 'hummed' for a minute. "Then ask yourself this. He might be ashamed, but are you?"

Something clicked, as if I had a clock inside of my skull. It made me think of the pocket watch, the way I'd identified Onyx as Seth. When I'd learned the truth, I hadn't run away. Hell, the closer I got to Seth's shadowy persona, the more addicted I became.

Maybe he was ashamed of his secret.

But was I?

"I'm not ashamed of any part of him," I said thoughtfully. "Not even a little bit."

"Then maybe you should tell him."

Again, I stared at the closet. *Tell him?* Onyx had made it abundantly clear that I wasn't worthy of belonging to him. I'd been a fool. There was no place for him at his side.

Except... if I forced him to choose...

"I need to go, Veronica."

"What? Already?"

"Yeah," I whispered, rising with determination. "I just remembered something I have to do."

****

190

Standing in front of the gold door was harder than it had ever been before.

But I'd made up my mind.

I wasn't about to back down.

Stepping through, my silvery flats made no noise on my descent. Corbin waited by the curtain, I hardly gave him a glance. With my mouth in a tight line, I scribbled down my name.

My dress was close to matching the curtain, a deep violet hue. Inside the main room, there was a clear, excited vibe.

I know the reason. The auction is tonight.

Glancing side to side, I spotted Roseli. The taller girl was clad in a flowing, wispy thing the color of burnt caramel. Her hair was wound up, elaborate and lovely. She looked proud, radiant as she awaited her fate.

If I follow her, I'll know where to go, what to do.

It wasn't a long wait.

Helm strolled into the den, standing tall with a surety possessed only by kings. He was as intimidating as Master Onyx, but no where near as thrilling. Looking over the crowd, he gave a curt jerk of his head.

Instantly, Roseli and a few other girls

began to follow him. I took a slow breath, trailing in among the tiny group slyly.

Onyx had told me I needed more training before being auctioned, but I had other ideas.

We moved down a hall I'd never explored, a path that opened up into the largest room so far. It was wide, brighter than the rest. Candles illuminated the round platform in the center, a place that drew my attention and held it.

That must be where we'll stand. We'll truly be like items in a showcase.

How right I was.

Helm motioned to Roseli, then one by one, the women began to ascend to the stage. I shook down to my marrow, avoiding the Master's gaze as I climbed the stairs. I thought he might say something about me being there, but he only smirked instead.

The second we were all lined up, a new group of collared slaves entered through the doors. I didn't know who they were, or why they were there.

"All of you are up for auction," Helm snapped at us. "Disrobe, then hand off your clothing."

Closing my eyes, I forced myself to relax. *Of course, of course they'd want that.*

The serene noise of fabric filled the air.

Looking down at myself, I peeled away the purple gown. I wouldn't show fear.

I was here on a mission.

When everyone stripped off their undergarments, I held my chin high and copied them. The air was cool, my nipples firming in seconds. My small strip of soft curls between my legs was the only protection I had. I realized the other women were all completely shaved.

Bending down, I offered my clothing to one of the slaves, watching her her collar glinted. "Your shoes as well," the brunette whispered.

Reluctantly, I crouched to tug off my flats. The first was uneventful, but the second...

Oh shit, I almost gasped out loud.

There, wrapped around one heel, was a tiny bandage. My wound had healed over the past few days, but I'd kept it covered out of habit.

If Seth saw it, would he connect the dots between Opal and me?

Handing off my shoes, sweat slid down the middle of my chest. *Calm down. It's just a little bandage. No way he'll notice.*

"Now," Helm called out, hands folded like a general. "All of you will kneel, and all of you will be silent. The Masters are about to arrive, assisting you in the grandest of your journeys. You will be sold tonight, you will become property. Do not speak unless spoken to, do not act unless instructed."

Drained from tension, I was grateful to crumble to my knees. Turning sideways, I saw the other girls all held a particular position; backs straight, chest thrust, hands on their thighs.

Had they received more proper training that I had? Licking my bottom lip, I emulated them as best as I could.

It felt strange, sitting so quietly, my body exposed to the eyes of any who wandered around the circular stage. We were elevated, chest level with any Master who wandered close.

For what felt like forever, we sat there. My muscles began to cramp.

Helm spoke softly with his group of collared women, and they began arranging chairs around the room. They'd barely finished when the first footsteps down the hall reached my ears.

Holding my breath, I looked up.

They entered with cool grace, heads held high and jaws squeezed tight. Each of them masked, each of them a vision of pure, male dominance. Any one of them would have made me squirm.

But only *he* could make me quiver to my

core.

Onyx entered like a shadow, his outfit as black as tar. Lifting his eyes, he scanned the stage, focusing on me instantly. His intensity, his calm disapproval, it stabbed me with absolute shame.

He's angry that I came here. He told me he wouldn't let me, that I needed more training.

Well, too bad, Master Onyx.

Too bad, Seth Hart.

Tonight I would find out what I needed to know. It would influence my decision to stay, or to leave and never return like I thought I had to.

Tonight, if he doesn't choose me, I'll walk away.

"Welcome, everyone." Helm spoke with a rumbling baritone, standing in front of the sitting men. "Tonight we have five girls for you to bid on, all of them lovely in their own ways. They've been trained, and they're ready to serve. Let us begin, shall we?"

He climbed on top of the stage, his boots clomping around us in a circle. "First, we have the beautiful Roseli." Helm reached down, stroking her shoulder. The girl flashed a tiny, pleased smile. "She's the most patient of the bunch, and easily the most obedient."

Wandering around the girls, Helm

talked about us as if we were livestock. The compliments were scant, and by the time he reached me, I was fidgeting from unease.

Reaching down, he grabbed my chin, forcing my head up towards the crowd. *No,* I thought desperately, *I don't want to look out there, I'm not ready to meet his eyes!*

"This girl," Helm grunted, "Is the most feisty of the lot. If you don't enjoy a slave who will require you to punish them often, I would avoid her." Freezing, I glanced up at Helm in surprise. His sneer was cruel, but his gaze was full of hunger. "I was thinking of taking her myself, honestly, as I *do* like girls who need a... firmer hand."

He let me go, but his threat stayed with me long after.

No, I can't go with Helm. If he picks me, I'll never come back here.

I'd draw blood to escape, if I had to.

I was spared from more of the cold man's commentary. He moved back through the line, then dropped down to the floor. Folding his arms, he nodded at the gathering. "I imagine you all want closer looks. Go ahead, help yourselves."

Closer looks?

The Masters rose in a gentle wave, coming to crash down upon all of us. They strolled around the stage, leaning close and talking to themselves. It was humiliating, yet still, it sent a rush through my blood.

That feeling grew ever higher when Onyx appeared before me. Staring down at my face, locking me with his fierce gaze, he spoke under his breath. "So, little jewel. You felt you were wiser than I, ready to auction yourself off in spite of my instructions?"

"No, I didn't think—"

His fingertips gripped either side of my face, crushing hard. "Yes, you didn't think. I actually debated with myself, you know. The thought about purchasing you." Those words had my heart soaring. "But," he went on, letting me go. "Now I know better. You are too defiant, too keen to break the rules."

He let me go, and I hung my head, sorrow chilling my blood and blackening my mood.

He might have chosen me, if I had just listened.

Onyx paused, fixated on something. Peeking over, I swore he was staring at my foot.

At my bandage.

A clawed hand strangled my lungs. *Shit. This is it.* He's going to notice, and then, everything will end.

But what did I care? Wasn't it over, anyway?

Together, he and I shared a long, heavy look. I couldn't twitch a limb, I was waiting for him to do... anything.

Crossing his arms, Onyx continued past me. He never said a word, there was no reaction that I could see. Had he not noticed that the cut was the very one he'd plucked glass from? That morning, he'd carried me away like I was a princess meant to be protected.

Watching him, I was more lost than ever.

He doesn't remember. That event meant more to me, than to him, after all.

This should have been a relief. It meant my secret was safe.

Why was I so defeated?

The Masters conversed among themselves. Staring hotly at my hands, I worked to smooth my breathing.

"So then," Helm bellowed, getting everyone's attention. "Let us begin the bidding. You should all recall how it works, simply raise a finger to bid. If we have multiple bidders, the price doubles for every digit. I don't expect anyone to lift a whole hand, but if so, you should make sure you're willing to spend that money." Climbing the stage, he gestured at the first girl. "Let's start with Roseli."

In their masks, with their stony mouths, it was impossible to see the Master's expressions. The subtle way they moved an arm, to wave a finger, showed a few wanted the tall woman.

I glimpsed the proud smile Roseli didn't bother to hide.

By the end, three of the men had lifted fingers, but the final one held up three. Helm grinned hungrily, sharing a look with Onyx. He seemed disappointed when the other man didn't look as delighted. "Well, there we go. Roseli, go join your new Master."

Easily she stood, entirely comfortable in her nudity and in her position here. Walking down the steps, she bent like a flower in the breeze at the feet of one of the sitting men.

Reaching down, he touched the back of her neck, whispering into her ear. Whatever he said, it made the girl beam.

The flicker of jealousy I felt boggled my mind.

Helm was nearby, his presence so close it made my skin itch. He touched the top of my head, and I jerked. "Let's talk about Opal. As I said, she's been a bit of trouble. However, she *was* so very, very eager during the session Onyx put her through the other night."

He made me remember the show I'd been a part of.

How I'd come multiple times for the crowd.

My blush was furious, sweat spreading between my shoulder blades.

"Who would like to bid on her?" he asked. I lifted my eyes, just enough to stare out at the emotionless sea of faces. At first, no one moved. On the nape of my neck, Helm gripped tighter, triumphant. "No one?"

No one? Peering at Onyx, I tried to read his mind.

Like a forgotten mountain, the dark man never moved.

Despair sank into my veins. *That's it. It's really over.* My effort had been wasted.

Onyx... Seth... they didn't want me.

"Then," Helm murmured, stroking the back of my ear. "I believe I'll happily—"

"No," Onyx cut him off. His hand was up, a finger pointed. "I'll bid on her. The little jewel belongs to me."

My lips spread in a relieved smile. I could have gotten up and danced. In that dim room, the lights brightened, colors saturating from my joy.

Were my eyes watering?

With my delirious grin, I tried to communicate my delight to Onyx. Oddly, he didn't seem pleased. If anything, his tense mouth hinted at something grim.

Above me, Helm gave my throat a

squeeze, then stepped away. "As you say, she is yours." Moving around, he eyed me with petulant longing. "Go to him, girl. You belong to Master Onyx now."

I belong to Master Onyx!

Standing on wobbly legs, I was amazed I made it down the steps without stumbling.

I'm his, I'm finally his.

Staring into his face, I dropped to my knees in my first display of fluid grace. Onyx placed his hand in his lap, but he didn't touch me. He didn't even try.

Unsure what was wrong, my smile broke. *Why is he so angry with me? Is it because I came here when he told me not to?*

It didn't matter. His anger would fade with time. All I cared was that he'd shown his true colors.

Seth—Onyx—he wanted me.

For the rest of the auction, I knelt there in heavy silence. It wasn't until everyone began to stand, striding from the room, that Onyx finally spoke.

"Come, Opal," he whispered. "We need to talk."

- Chapter Thirteen -
Naomi

One of the woman handed me the clothing I'd arrived in. Redressing, sliding my feet into my shoes, I rushed to tag along after Onyx.

Together we walked down the hall. I stayed just behind, watching his heels. His whole body was tight, an elastic at its limit. It actually scared me.

I expected us to head off to a private room. What I didn't predict was that Onyx would lead us to the main area, and once there, continue on through the curtains.

Pulling up short, I gaped after his vanishing back.

Oh, no.

I knew what had happened. Staring down at my flats, then back again, I grasped the situation firmly.

He knows.

Like a prisoner heading for the electric chair, I walked through the drapes.

Upstairs, pushing past the door, I looked around. I didn't see him, not at first.

"No regard for my rules, not even now. Right, Ms. Starling?"

I spun, finding Seth sitting on the couch in the foyer. His legs were crossed, one arm on the back of the seat. In his other hand, he held his black mask. He turned it, as if he was seeing it for the first time.

Lifting his head, he rolled his cold sapphire eyes over to me.

Shaking like a leaf, I reached up, touching my own disguise.

This is it.

The game was done. He'd figured it all out.

Even so, I hesitated, enjoying the last few seconds where our lives in the dungeon below didn't have to exist, here, in the real world.

The mask came away in my hands, heavy as a boulder dragging me beneath the waves.

"That isn't it," I said. "I just—I was curious."

Tilting his head, a cruel smile grew. "And was your curiosity sated?"

"It was." Hanging my head, I reached up to untie my hair. The elaborate curls fell apart. Their limp, shapeless mess seemed fitting.

Looking away, his forehead crinkled. His mask was set on the couch. "Why did you keep going back?" he asked. His emotions restrained, Seth approached me. "Why did you return so many times?"

Flushing crimson, I looked away.

He glowered, raw fury finally leaking into his hot words. "Corbin will take you home. Gather anything of yours you brought. I have no more need of you."

Though I had once expected such a reaction from him... I was still shocked. My hair whipped when I twisted back. "What do you mean? I haven't finished the mural!"

"I don't care!" His features creased, a rage that had been slithering below the surface exploding. "*I do not care anymore!* You broke my rules, Ms. Starling. Again and again, you broke them, flaunted them! You put myself, my clients, everything at risk! Do you understand what a contract means? Did you even *read* it?"

I had no response, his anger had stolen my voice.

Seth came forward, and so help me, I shrank. He ripped the mask from my fingers, throwing it at a far wall. "I don't need you coming back here, I don't *want* you coming back. Do you hear me?"

Tiny, explosive bursts of sound left my lips. He was terrifying, but as I let him rant, my own fury was cresting. Who was he to tell me I was wrong? He'd coerced me into misbehaving!

With his hot words, dark promises and

quick fingers...

Seth had led me astray from the start.

"Your rules are pointless," I said. "What we were doing down there... what we had..." My knuckles went white. "Just because you suddenly realized that I was Opal, you want to end it?"

Still as a pond, his words were a gritty whisper. "Suddenly? You think I only just found out?"

I faltered. "Of course." Lifting my foot, I tilted it sideways. "You saw the bandage, wasn't that how you knew?"

His hand came up, as if he'd strike me, but he only ruffled his hair. "Do you think I'm so stupid? I knew you were Opal from the very first night!"

Was I sinking into the floor? Nothing was stable anymore. My voice was far away. "I don't understand."

"Cameras," he spat, pointing around the room. "I have security cameras set up to protect me from thieves." His eyes flashed. "I never expected to catch something else."

Slowly, my head moved side to side. The small, black lenses were nearly invisible until he pointed them out. Cold shame burned my body upwards from the root.

He knew from day one.

I went to speak, then had to start over when only dry air escaped. "Then why." *He knew all along.* "Why kick me out now?"

"I told you. You didn't follow my rules."

"But—why *now?* I'd been breaking the rules each time I went down there!"

Seth stood tall, his broad chest flexing through the open front of his shirt. "You forced my hand. I told you not to go to the auction. I *don't... like...*" Each word was punctuated. "Having my hand forced."

He made a fist, and I surprised myself by stepping forward. His eyes flickered, shocked as well. "I know what you like. You liked dominating me, you liked making me beg and cry and scream!" I moved again, and when he didn't back down, we came chest to chest. "You, *Master Onyx,* like to fuck with people's heads until they don't even know how to feel anymore!"

He looked down his nose at me, lip curling in a feral display. I was breathing heavily, fighting back the tears of anger and unfairness that clawed at my eyes.

Seth asked, "Are you trying to upset me?"

The look in his eyes was carving into my center. Strings of scalding passion, born from our frustration, our confusing needs, yanked us closer. When he leaned down, just a hair, I

206

inhaled.

His eyes widened, mimicking the tension—the sudden rush—that had infected me.

How had we gotten here?

"If I upset you," I whispered, "What will you do? Punish me?"

Knotting his eyebrows, he scowled. "You'd like that, wouldn't you?" Seth brought his gloved fingers near my cheek, and my small gasp gave me away. "Yes," he chuckled. "You want me to make you pay."

Do I want that?

His suggestion stoked the wicked, corrupt part of me. The twisted thing he'd helped grow. Seth had become such a natural at working my body, heating me up until my pussy was dripping beyond belief.

He stared me down, his sneer firm and solid. I licked my lips, trying to come up with an answer that would prove I wasn't so weak.

So... desperate.

I never found one.

His lips crashed onto mine, sealing away my pitiful denial. Tangling my hair up, he crushed me to him, bending me towards the floor. It was something out of a movie, if movies would ever dare play a perverse story like ours.

He's finally kissing me.

The thought was a distant prickle.

But he also kicked me out.

His tongue curled, dominating mine, pushing it down as he grazed me with his teeth. I'd fantasized that his lips would feel wonderful, but I'd been wrong.

They were so much more than that.

Wrapping my hands around his shoulders, I started to kiss him back, but Seth wouldn't have it. Trapping my wrists, he forced them behind me, leaving me at his mercy. A frail whimper bubbled up.

Breaking the kiss, Seth ensured there was a gap between us. Pathetically, I tried to reach him, but he just laughed and pulled me away. "You're wrong," he said flatly. "You *ache* to be punished. What a predictable girl."

I was slow to respond. There was too much cotton in my skull, but eventually, I met his eyes. "Then I guess you fell for a predictable girl, *Master.*"

His mask—his real, invisible mask—cracked.

Seth shoved me away, I had to grab the couch for balance. Through the messy strands of my hair, I narrowed my eyes on him. The air was cloying between us. This situation wasn't one that we'd expected to find ourselves in.

Through the golden door, voices murmured.

Snapping a look towards the noise, he shoved around me. Recovering his mask from the couch, he covered his face. "Get out of here, Ms. Starling. Our game is over. Both of us walk away with nothing."

A hard knot gripped my heart. *Nothing? He can't mean that.*

Straightening, I shook my head. "What about the recommendation letter? You promised I could have it!"

Frosty eyes studied me, unfazed. Our moment of passion could have been a mere dream. "As I said, you should have read your contract. My promise is voided. We're done here."

Turning away, he stalked down the nearby hall.

There was no farewell.

Not for me.

****

The drive was tense, the lights of the city going unseen.

I sat in the back, brooding over whether to be angry, or to be miserable.

Both. I'll just be both.

"I'm sorry this happened," Corbin mumbled over the sound of the engine.

Sitting up, I leaned forward, trying to catch his eye in the mirror. "Did you know about everything?"

"You mean you sneaking into the dungeon? Yes, of course I knew."

"But you never told him."

"No," he agreed somberly. "I did not. He discovered it on the security tapes, himself."

Biting my lip, I sighed. "I hope you didn't get in trouble."

He glanced at me in the mirror. "I was under no obligation to inform him. I didn't break his rules."

His rules.

"Can you explain to me why he was so pissed off? It can't possibly matter so much if I know about that place, about what he does."

"Of course it matters." He steered us around a curve in the road. "Mr. Hart runs a private event, a place people can go to and be someone else entirely. Secrecy is the utmost importance to him, and you risked exposing him, and others, by returning to that place every night. You were never invited."

I shook my head, not understanding. "How can they not know he's Seth? Isn't it obvious?"

"Was it obvious to you?"

Blushing, I sat back in my seat.

Corbin's eyes softened. "Even if they knew, they would never say. He knows who they all are, and that is much more powerful. It's part of the condition of joining, they must sign over their identification and a privacy agreement. They never meet Seth Hart, they only ever meet me."

I pictured Corbin sitting behind Seth's desk, and had to smile.

"Yes, it's clear I work for him," he said. "But the house isn't in his name, people can't simply look it up and find out he's the owner. Any who would get as far as attending the events have already signed away their rights. They'd risk scandal by stirring trouble."

I propped my head on the window, closing my eyes.

"Don't be too offended," he said gently. "Mr. Hart is a unique man. I admit, I've never seen him so enamored with anyone before. You really left an impression on him."

"Too bad it ended like this, then," I laughed bitterly.

"Yes," he admitted. "It is too bad."

The car pulled up outside my apartment, lighting up the garbage cans and chasing off some cats. Climbing out, I glanced back at Corbin. "Tell him I'm really sorry. I didn't mean to mess everything up."

He smiled, nodding his head, but it felt... false.

He knows it won't matter.

I watched the car until the glow of it vanished around the street corner. Turning, I passed the garbage, spotting a dead roach. The sight made my guts squeeze, driving another nail into my morbid mood.

Frowning severely, I limped into my small, familiar apartment.

It felt more empty than it ever had before.

- Chapter Fourteen -
Seth

Back and forth, I prowled through the halls of my home. My fingers dug into the air, choking unseen things.

How could this happen?

Crossing into the kitchen, I slammed the backdoor open. The night air was cool on my skin.

How could I LET this happen?

That was what it came down to. I'd been a fucking fool. The minute I'd seen Naomi on the footage, sneaking through the door, I should have stormed to her room and thrown her out.

But I hadn't.

What had stopped me?

Chlorine tainted the air where I paced by the pool. Water sloshed gently, tinkling like music, the green lights turning my skin an awful shade.

Lifting a hand, I studied my palm. It still smelled like her hair, that intoxicating cinnamon scent of hers.

Chuckling sourly, I ran my hand down my face. *It's my fault.*

I had all the power, but I hadn't exercised it until the very end. She'd slid under my skin, growing until she was a part of me.

Like a god damn tumor.

My rage wasn't enough to make me believe that.

Naomi... she'd appeared beneath my stairs, dancing in the shadow world I'd created for my own dark pleasure. Seeing her there, the first night, I'd been intrigued. I hadn't known it was her.

Then, hours later, scanning the footage as my insomnia did its usual dance...

I'd seen her.

That woman, she'd slipped into one of the masks I kept on hand for emergencies—I'd had guests before who lost their own on the way to the mansion—and she'd crept down the hall and through the door.

From there, I'd battled with my irritation, and my curiosity. She'd been a delight to toy with. I loved how she'd jump when I'd slyly approach her as she painted. I was addicted to the small gasps she made.

That had only grow when I'd heard the sounds she made beneath my house.

Connecting Opal and Naomi had been tragic.

It had also been wonderful.

When she'd seen me tonight with my mask off, there'd been no shock. That had told me *her* secret; she'd known I was Onyx.

She'd *known*, and the girl had come back every time.

Why? I wondered, crouching down to brush the warm water. *What kept her coming back?* The obvious answer was that she'd wanted the things I was doing to her. She'd been so invested, obsessed, that she'd risked everything for another taste.

Crushing my fingers, I splashed my hand in the pool. *Stupid girl.* Shaking my hand, I dried it on my pants. *But I'm stupid, too.*

How long would I have kept this charade up?

I'd tried to coerce her with more art jobs. I'd longed to keep our game going.

Closing my eyes, I sighed.

Naomi had wanted me to collar her. It was an act I'd never done before.

Fuck, the way she'd reacted when she was worried I would let someone else buy her. I couldn't forget how I'd crushed her into the rug, our eyes flashing like diamonds across from each other. I'd seen her fear, then, and it had given me pause.

But even after facing my fury, she'd come back.

She was insane.

And I *loved* that.

How could I begrudge her? I was no different.

Snorting, I stood, walking towards the house.

To me, control was everything. But once I'd dominated a girl, the excitement—the drive —it always faded. I'd never taken a personal submissive. I'd trained many, but that was all.

I'd never wanted someone.

Not until...

No, I snapped at myself. Snarling, I stomped into the main entrance room. *You can't have her. She doesn't listen, she'll never fully break.*

Slowing down, I stared up at the railing above. The mural there was a storm of colors, raging and reminding me of my own emotions. It had a subtle quality to it, but that was easily lost if you focused on the black clouds and grey hints.

This was what Naomi had painted.

I'd told her to do anything, and she'd created this explosion of inner turmoil. It was more fitting than she could realize.

Naomi was wild, she was free. Yet she had a softer part, a velvet center that ached for me to stroke it and cup it in my palm. She *craved* domination, it was built into her blood.

And yet, someone like her...

She can't be tamed.

I stood straight, saturated in cold understanding. *That's right.* Again, I studied the painting; the reason I'd been attracted to her in the first place. *Naomi is wild, she wants to bend, but she'll never fully yield.*

And that...

That was why I wanted her.

It was what separated her from all the other subs I'd encountered. Naomi had life, fire, and the way she resisted excited me.

The first time we'd been alone, she'd kicked me. Bit and fussed even as I gagged her. The imagery, even now, had my cock growing hard.

And tonight, after I'd demanded she leave, she'd stood her ground. She'd stared me down, and when I'd risen to meet her, we'd exploded in a furious kiss.

Touching my lips, I closed my eyes, shivering.

I wanted to taste her again. I wanted...

I wanted her back.

There was a maddening lust in me. A desire to hunt her down, claim her until she could remember nothing but my name as she screamed it over and over. I itched to fill her every crevice. Even breathing would be secondary.

Turning, I stared at the front door.

I'm not done with her, I realized, clenching my fingers.

I would do whatever it took to make her mine again.

But this time, it would be on *my* terms.

- Chapter Fifteen -
Naomi

It had been several days since I'd last seen Seth.

Even thinking of him was painful.

I'd tried to push past the depression, but the sadness... the defeat... it ruled my world. I'd lost access to a wonderful, enticing man who'd opened my mind and body to a whole other level of pleasure.

I'd also lost the ticket into the college of my dreams.

For the first time, the day after he'd yelled at me, I'd actually sat and read the contract. The clause was very specific: break the rules, and my rewards were forfeit.

No money.

No letter.

What was I going to do? How did I recover from this?

My phone buzzed, ripping me back to the present. I almost didn't answer, but the sound of another voice was appealing. "Hey Mom," I mumbled, falling backwards onto my couch-bed.

"Is something wrong, Naomi? You sound... off."

My smile was sour, I was glad my mother couldn't see it. "No, everything is fine," I whispered, rubbing my eyes with my forearm. The tears came suddenly, insistent as they rolled down my cheeks. "Everything is just great, Mom. So great."

"Naomi..."

Rolling on my side, I looked out over my drab apartment. The sight of it was too much. Just like that, all I wanted to do was get away from this city. I could start over. Besides, it wasn't as if I had anything keeping me here.

Not anymore.

"Mom, I was thinking, is the offer to go home still there?"

"Honey, listen—"

A sharp knock on the door startled me. Sitting up, my brain somersaulted. I stared across the room.

The sound came again, demanding.

"Hang on," I said from the corner of my mouth. "I'll call you right back." Ignoring the frustrated, confused words my mother made, I hung up.

Sliding off the bed, I approached my door warily. *Who could it be?* For a moment, I debated not answering at all. The rap of knuckles returned. That time, I pulled the handle.

220

In a white button-down and faded jeans, a look I'd never seen him sport before, Seth stood on my front step. He looked down on me, as penetrating as ever.

"Seth." His name came out in a puff of air. "I—what are you doing here?"

He didn't blink, didn't move. "Can I come in?"

Unsure what to do, my flesh hungering instantly for the man I'd never expected to see again, I slid a heel backwards. Once he'd entered, I closed the door gently. Seth was studying my tiny, messy apartment. My cheeks turned cherry red. "Uh, sorry about the place, I was..."

"Ms. Starling," he said, spinning to face me. The seriousness in his expression froze me where I was. "I came here to offer you something."

The surrealism of this encounter was fading. Seth had been enraged with me the last time we'd seen each other. What had changed? Why was he messing with my head like this?

My mouth twisted at the corners. "You took everything I wanted away from me. What are you playing at here?"

The intensity in his stare burned at my fucking center. I knew those eyes, that ferocity.

On impulse, I clenched my thighs together.

221

He said, very slowly, "I spent some time considering how we left things." The reminder of our fight didn't calm my nerves. "Perhaps I was too hasty."

"Too hasty?" I replied numbly.

His smile crossed into a wicked promise. "If you truly want another chance, like you begged for so dearly, I'm willing to give it to you."

Moving my mouth, I sought to make sense of the emotions waging in me. Excitement... relief... and doubt. "You'd still write me that letter? If this is a trick, I--"

Lifting a hand, he silenced me. That would have been enough, but Seth bent closer, corralling me against the wall in a split second. "This offer doesn't come easy. Ms. Starling, if you agree to this, there will be conditions."

Conditions. Thinking about that damn contract, I narrowed my eyes. "More rules?"

I saw his teeth. "*One* rule."

My heart thumped in a constant, rising tide. Seth pressed his palm to the wall, blocking me in with his body—his heat. I could smell him, and that scent had me wobbling.

"Returning to my home comes with a price. You spent so much time with me behind that special door... surely you know my taste for punishment. And surely we *both* know how much you enjoy it."

222

In my throat, my breathing hitched. Like I had a portal into his twisted mind, I could imagine every single thing he was. Worse, the arousal was radiating out of me.

Was I so damaged, so longing for more, that even the mere mention of his torture had me growing wet?

Swallowing, I said, "Just tell me what you want."

Grinning, he took a slow inhale. "I want you to let me have my way with you. Allow me to punish you the way a Dom would reprimand his sub. If you don't back down, no matter *how hard* I go at you..." His fingers cupped my cheek, and it took everything I had not to lean forward and kiss him. "Then, dear Opal." My heart jumped at that name. "You may have your wish. You'll get your letter."

The huskiness in his tone said volumes. If I went back, Seth would be allowed to do whatever he wanted to me. I'd seen some of his tools, felt the hot burn of his palms. How devious would he be with me without boundaries?

What if I *couldn't* handle it?

Seth was watching me closely. The hunger in his face said he knew why my cheeks were so flushed. Clearing my throat, I met his eyes as calmly as I could. "How much time do I have to think this over?"

Backing away from me, he smoothed his jacket. "Until tonight. If you want this chance, just message Corbin. Once you reach my home, there will be no going back."

His threat curled inside my lower belly. "I understand."

"Good." With one more look around my apartment, Seth circled towards the door. "Don't take my offer lightly. This is no game." Peering back at me, his eyes were heated. "I look forward to hearing you beg again."

And then he was gone.

Breathing out like a deflated balloon, I fell onto my bed. Standing was impossible. Seth had left, and he'd taken my strength with him. *Another chance.* The phrase was so nice.

If only it didn't come with a price.

Brushing my hair back, I looked at my palms, flexing my fingers. I'd never expected to see Seth again. But the opportunity to go back to the erotic, dark world he'd opened my heart to... it was immensely tempting.

He acted like he was sure I'd agree.

His parting words had made my heart drum madly. And was he wrong for being so cocky? I *needed* that letter, but he had acted like I needed something else.

I had to wonder, if I did go back, would it be for the letter, or would that just be my excuse?

It scared me, how little I knew myself anymore.

Standing up, I looked for my phone.

****

Corbin said nothing as we drove.

The tires crunched, rolling us along the curved roads up the Hollywood hills. The sky was too bright, it didn't fit with the hurdle I was about to face.

Unable to handle the crushing silence, I said, "How has he been lately?"

The driver glanced at me in the mirror. After a second, he looked away again.

Sinking into the seat, I hugged myself until I was a tight knot. Corbin's silence felt... forced. Had Seth instructed him not to speak to me?

If the goal was to give me a sense of hopelessness, it wouldn't work. I'd decided to return to Seth's home, and I'd done it for myself.

No matter how this ended, I had a chance at gaining something. I still believed that when life offered such things, you had to snatch them up.

Seth had made the offer, but the control wasn't all his.

No one had forced me into this car.

No one but me.

The gates appeared, and my chest went cold. Sitting up, I listened to the ringing in my ears as Corbin parked the car. He came around, helping me out, but still never looking at me.

Then, as I started to break away, he brushed my wrist. "Good luck," Corbin whispered.

With a weak smile, I headed towards the front door.

The place hadn't changed. I don't know why I had expected it to. Though just a few days had passed, it felt like a lifetime.

I didn't see Seth; my eyes had gone straight up, taking in the familiar, unfinished mural I'd spent almost two weeks working on. A part of me, deep down, twanged with regret. I wanted to run up to that painting, to finish what I'd started.

The incomplete state of it was painful.

"So you decided to come."

Jerking up straight, I watched Seth as he turned on the couch. He'd been facing away, and now, I could see his strong back straining against the smooth surface of his suit. It was a rich blue, deeper than his eyes.

Eyes that burned into me with expectation.

Clearing my throat, I stepped further into the room. I didn't want to look as unsure as I felt. *Face your fears head on.* Besides, what was I scared of? Seth?

Yes.

I guess I was.

Folding my arms, I said, "Are you actually surprised?"

His lips didn't smile, but his eyes did. "Not many people would walk willingly into danger."

Danger. My heart throbbed, but I pushed it down. "I already know what you're capable of." *And you know how much I enjoy it.* My own thoughts had me blushing.

Seth tilted his jaw, reminding me how atrociously handsome he was. "You *think* you know what I'm capable of, Ms. Starling." Pushing off the couch, he strolled my way with a confident sway. His hands were deep in his pockets, pulling my attention to his hips—his belt—and making me imagine what rested beneath.

That body...

That amazingly thick cock.

Dazed, I inched my heel back when he was mere inches away. Seth stood over me, a shadow in his smile. He whispered, "You're naive to believe you know what I can do. What I *want* to do. All men have monsters inside of them."

"Yes, and I've met yours. A few times," I said, nodding at the golden door.

"No," he chuckled. "You've only glimpsed mine." One hand slid into view, and I thought he would touch me... but he only straightened his tie. "Knowing that, are you still sure you're ready to face it in the dark? Unrestrained, no limits... no backing down?"

I couldn't stop watching how he stroked his tie. My mouth was dry; I swallowed, then narrowed my eyes at him. His cockiness was frustrating. It drove me crazy how easily he had my lower belly purring.

Steeling myself, I breathed deep. "Is this really the only way to get back in your good graces?"

Seth's fingers paused on his tie, choking it. "Yes."

"Then I'm not walking away." I dug for every fiber of confidence inside of me. "I'm not going to throw away this chance."

"Even if what I do to you leaves you in pieces?" he asked softly.

Astoundingly, I didn't react. "You wouldn't do that to me."

He hesitated, uncertainty swimming through his eyes. Then it was gone, and Seth motioned us towards the golden door. "Let's not waste any time, brave girl."

My feet were as heavy as anchors. I didn't feel them while I walked. I didn't even feel my hands at the ends of my arms. Faced with the moment, knowing that we were about to descend into that place where I'd done so many, many sexual things...

It left me breathless.

Worse, we were going down there as ourselves. Always before, I'd had the safety of my mask. I could cloak myself in secrecy, pretend I was someone else. But now, we wouldn't be Onyx and Opal.

Seth meant to have his way with me as himself.

Whatever happened after this... I wouldn't be able to shake free of it.

Naomi—me—I'd experience everything.

"Go on," he said, opening the door.

Perching at the top of the stairs, my molars throbbed; my jaw was locked. I passed close to him, catching his intoxicating scent. I had a vision of myself swooning, tumbling down the steps until I was just a broken heap.

Would that be worse than what he had planned for me?

"Go," he said. Every hair on my body became a solid spear.

The first step was the hardest. The rest came easier, like the momentum was carrying me forward. There were lights on the walls, but they did little to brighten the mood.

How did I get here? I wondered, listening to my shoes thump on the carpet. *And why is this so foreboding?* I'd already let Seth tie me up, he'd teased me, tortured me...

Fucked me till I was ready to pass out.

So why was this so different?

He said all men have monsters inside of them.

Was he right, that I had no clue what he was truly capable of? Was my intuition preparing me for something terrible, and that was why my hands were shaking?

The curtain rose up. For once, there was no gentle hum of voices on the other side. Seth stood close behind me, stopping all chances of escape. I'd said I was ready—said I could handle whatever he had in store for me.

In a way, I was glad he was there to block me. Fighting the urge to bolt up the stairs was hard enough. "Ms. Starling, are you ready?"

Unable to look away from the curtain, I nodded slowly.

"Do you want me to give you one more chance to back away?" he asked.

I parted my lips. "No."

"Good." His fingers grazed my elbow,

making me jump. "I don't think I could let you leave. Not when I'm so close to getting to taste you again."

Shivering, I half-turned, but Seth pushed me through the curtain. The shove made me stumble, though it wasn't rough; my knees were simply too stiff, my balance lost in my growing anxiety.

The main area was unsettling. With no people, it felt haunted. Spinning, I watched Seth as he waited. I *knew* he was waiting, and I had an idea what for. Licking my lower lip, I said, "Where do you want me to go?"

His head nodded down the hall. "I think you have some idea."

Facing the dark corridor, the memory of the night that Seth—Onyx—had brought me forward for my first training session wormed in my guts. It made me warm, and it nipped at my confused brain.

He was right.

I knew exactly where we were going.

- Chapter Sixteen -
Naomi

Clenching my hands, I walked stiffly down the hall. Behind me, Seth followed, saying nothing. He didn't stop me when I approached the room he'd first tied me up in. The place he'd shown he could break me.

What would he do to me now?

In the center of the room, I turned towards him. He swung the door closed, the metal clicking as it locked. I doubted we'd be interrupted, but the extra barrier added to my nerves.

His slight smile said he knew—and that he liked it.

"So," he said, undoing the buttons on his jacket. "Here we are."

It was such a meaningless statement, I almost laughed. "Yes. Here we are."

"You're calmer than I thought you'd be." He draped his jacket over a chair. Beneath, his white shirt was out of place. Down here, Seth shouldn't have been allowed such purity. "Are you really not scared? Or is it that... maybe... you're looking forward to what I have planned for you?"

My tongue stuck to the roof of my

232

mouth. There was too much truth in his observation. I did want this, even if it was in a deep, low part of me that was fucked up. A sliver that was tempted by the sordid and erotic things Seth could do to me.

His eyebrows arched. "No response?"

Lifting my chin, I frowned. "Isn't it enough of an answer that I'm here?"

"You're here, I'm just trying to figure out why." Peeling his sleeves back, he came my way. "Is it because of the letter... or is there more?"

When he was a foot away, I tightened up from toe to jaw. "What do you mean?"

Laughing under his breath, he shrugged. "Ms. Starling, do you *want* me to destroy you?" In the low lights, his eyes went black. "Do you ache for my punishment? For how I can make you sweat... make you scream and beg until your voice is raw?"

He was on me, a towering, intimidating beast that pawed at some instinctual desire. It didn't matter if he was right.

I didn't want to admit anything.

"Lift your hands," he snapped, so crisp his tone could cut diamonds.

Sweat coated my palms. Whether it was defiance or nerves, I didn't move an inch. The look in his eyes was soaked with wild passion. He *wanted* me to fight. I was giving him exactly what he'd hoped for.

In a flash, he snatched up my arms, wrenching them over my head. *It's just like last time,* I thought, struggling in his grip. Seth was pure muscle, he held me easily with one wide hand as he locked my wrists in the cuffs dangling from the ceiling.

Stepping back, he smiled. "Still so quiet."

Yanking at the shackles, I glared at him. "It's not like there's much for me to say. You made it clear, you're going to do what you want."

"Yes. And I'll remind you that you agreed."

Without a rebuttal, I bit the inside of my cheek.

From his pocket, Seth slid something metallic into the light. I thought it was his watch, but the shape was wrong.

My heart jerked.

A knife!

"Wait," I said, eyeing the wicked blade. "You can't use that on me." My smile was shaky, nervous. "You wouldn't actually hurt me, right?"

I didn't like the coolness in his stare. "Now that you're strung up, unable to escape, you finally wonder about that?" Turning the knife, Seth ran it along the sleeve of my shirt. I'd worn jeans and a basic, yellow blouse. Through the material, the metal was all I could focus on.

Hooking the knife in the throat of my shirt, Seth smiled and said, "Here's your answer."

Two things happened at once: I screamed.

And the shirt shredded away.

Gasping frantically, I watched as he cut my clothing into strips. The shirt vanished, drifting to the floor in a puddle. Next, my jeans were sawed at, my legs exposed to the air. Seth was efficient, he acted with familiarity as he worked.

My relief over not being harmed made it easy to forget I was almost naked. The sound of my bra strap popping pulled me back to reality.

I felt the air from the motion of his hand. It tickled over my breasts, bringing them to attention. I wanted to curse my body; it responded to Seth's presence, I was hyper aware of how close he was to my nipples.

In seconds, they firmed to the point of throbbing.

Kneeling, he cut my panties away without flourish. It baffled me how he could switch between business and the lusty, beastly side I saw deep in his eyes.

Dangling as I was, my calves burned from keeping me upright. Taking me by the shoulders, he let his lips come near my cheek. "There, now we're ready to begin."

Abruptly he spun me, and for a moment, I was confused. There, just feet away, I stared at a naked woman. She was flushed, straining on her toes with her neck pulsing madly. Her lips were red and thick.

Such an erotic sight was strange when it was combined with the fear in her eyes.

Eyes just like mine.

And then I knew.

A mirror.

Seth had tied me up in front of a mirror. I'd experienced being gagged, as well as blindfolded, but being forced to watch myself was a new level of kink. I saw my nostrils flare as I inhaled sharply.

At my shoulder, Seth was smirking.

"Lovely," he said, "Isn't it?" Reaching down, he brushed my bare hip. "I wanted you to watch me work. You'll see everything I do to you, Ms. Starling."

Even now, he calls me that. It was impersonal. How could he be so distant while I was nude and vulnerable? *Maybe that's what he needs.* Seth didn't require a physical mask.

He'd been wearing one all along.

Seth wandered over to dig inside a wooden chest. When he returned, he held a long spool of glossy white rope. "I've wanted to do this to you since I first brought you in here, Ms. Starling."

Hooking the strands through his fingers, he unwound it. My eyes widened, trying to imagine what he was going to do to me. My mind was cruel, so I finally gave up and just asked. "What will you do with those?"

Lifting an eyebrow, Seth snapped the rope. The sound of the whip-crack was felt in my bones. "Many things, my dear."

In the mirror, I caught the dark excitement in his glistening blue eyes.

He draped the rope over my shoulders and down my ribs, sinking the ends deep down the valley of my breasts. Both pieces wove behind me, over my spine, only to reappear.

I never would have guessed that Seth was an artist. I'd known he appreciated my painting, but this was something else entirely.

Soft nylon, the texture was pleasant where it touched me. Again, he wound the ends across my flesh. Soon, my chest was circled tight, the ropes pushing my breasts out in obscene, swollen shapes.

In the mirror, I saw the deep pink color of my nipples, watched them grow harder as I stared.

"You appreciate the art, I take it," he said. Chuckling, he rolled a fingertip down my shoulder until he brushed the sensitive tip of my right nipple. Both of us watched how I whimpered; I couldn't control my reaction. "Yes," he purred, "The ropes draw sensation to the areas they choke. You'll feel everything more intensely."

How could this get *more* intense?

Coiling the ropes around my waist, he layered them around my hips. Lower he went, binding my knees, my ankles. When he came back up, tucking the cord between the V of my legs, I gasped. "What are you doing?"

"Whatever I want. I thought that was clear." The rope was yanked, threading through my slit and the cleft of my ass. It nestled intimately, and as I shifted helplessly, I bit back a moan. In spite of everything, the bondage was turning me on.

Seth hoisted the rope upwards until I felt him tying it behind my shoulder blades. The knot he'd formed between my thighs was wide. It ran along my lower lips, digging into my pussy.

With how my legs were bound, ankles clasped and knees touching, I could hardly move.

But I could wiggle—why had he left me any freedom at all?

"You're so gorgeous when you're trapped," he whispered, lips kissing my earlobe. My eyes shut, pleasure forcing me to flutter into a delightful daze. It wasn't something he'd let me escape into, though. Seth had plans.

He decided to remind me of them.

One hand came down, slapping sharply on my nipple. "Ah!" I shouted, staring at him in shock. He did it again, harder, and I convulsed. Stretching forward, my hips arched on impulse. The pressure on the ropes shifted, the massive knot digging into my pussy.

Right into my clit.

Gasping, I twitched violently, but that just made the soft nylon tighten more. Seth had tied the ropes in such a way that any movement I made caused the knot to slide deeper, rougher, unrelenting over my swollen nub.

"How?" I blurted, fighting not to move any more. Already, the sensation of having my pussy rubbed was making me wet.

"Do you like it?" Bending low, he nuzzled my chest. Tingles erupted down my spine. Blood had engorged my breasts, everything he did was felt ten-fold. "When you move, the ropes squeeze harder. In turn... they feel even better. I can already smell how excited you are."

Blushing at his observation, I started

239

panting. Sweat glided down my ribs. "Untie me, it's too much!"

"You've forgotten our agreement." With both hands he thumbed my nipples. I braced myself, throwing my head back. Willing myself to freeze, I flexed my toes until they cramped. "Watching you fight gets my cock rock hard, did you know that?"

His words were too much.

With pressure mounting in my belly, I thrust into the knots. They did their job, gliding over my clit again and again, sending me into new spasms. Resisting was impossible; at this rate, the ropes would make me come.

Humping the air, I moaned like I was in heat. Fuck, I *felt* like I was in heat! Seth had my body thrumming, the bonds forcing pleasure out of me whether I wanted it or not.

Why am I fighting this? I wondered. *I can't remember why I'm resisting.*

I'd been depressed when Seth had banished me from his home. I'd wanted more of him, more of this. Now, I was getting it in spades.

What gall did I have to complain?

Seth had vanished, but I didn't notice. Not until the strands of leather slapped over my ass. Squealing, I flooded with pain and blinding warmth from grinding into the ropes.

Behind me, there was fire—the kind that

seared.

In front of me, there was fire as well. But this one brought glory, it licked at my thighs and drove me mad.

"Fuck," he hissed, uncharacteristically crass. "Seeing you writhe is addicting."

I bit my tongue as another lash hit my skin. Colors rolled through my skull. In the mirror, I saw how I glowed. Sweat poured everywhere, my hair sticking to my forehead.

I can't take this!

The flogger kept on, assaulting me with precision. Seth knew where to attack, leaving me lost in a sea that ate away at my mind. Pain, pleasure, what was the difference?

"It's too much!" All the rebellion fled me. It flooded away as easily as the juices from my pussy. "I give up!" I cried. "No more, you win, just stop!"

Seth circled around, facing me. I hung my head, gasping for air, but he gripped my chin and pulled me back up. He was so close, I saw every eyelash over his explosive stare. "Sweetness, you misunderstand. This isn't about winning or making you beg. This is about what *I* want... and I want to make you sing."

For the first time, I saw a flash of the monster that slept inside of him.

Bending low, he ran his tongue over one sensitive nipple. I keened loudly, thrusting my hips forward as my thighs clenched. This was true control—Seth commanded every inch of my body.

My mind.

Nothing was safe from him. If he wanted to leave me in a shattered pile, he could. We both knew that, now.

I imagine he always knew.

I was foolish, I thought through my haze. *I thought I could handle him.*

Seth was not someone meant to be handled.

Only survived.

He nibbled my breast, thumbing the other with growing need. His torso rocked against my hip, the hard shape of his erection bumping me. That added to my lust, hot ripples running from my heart to my cunt.

"Do you want to come?" he whispered, two fingers outlining the rope as he ran his palm down my belly. He brushed right above my pussy, flicking the soaked knot gently. Still, I felt the echo of his thump through the rope, right against my clit.

My lungs expanded, pushing my ribs to their limit.

Again, he snapped the rope. "Do you *want to come?*" It was a demand, words that carved right into my soul. If someone had opened me up right then, they'd have found the perverse question tattooed forever in my flesh.

Did I *want* to come?

This went beyond want.

My whole being was raging, heated and sweating and so alive it was hurting me. The unrelenting rubbing over my pussy was maddening. The throbbing in my trapped breasts kept me awake.

Seth curled his hand in my hair, forcing me to look at him. Even his grip, causing my scalp to burn, was making me swim in delirious arousal. "Say it. Say you want to come. Beg for me. Show me how much you want this."

Everything he spoke was a command. I was foggy, but even so, my mind snatched at what he'd said. *He wants me to show him?* Hadn't I done that already? Wasn't being here enough?

I'd risked my future by coming to this place each and every night. I'd broken the rules, fought with everything to make him see I wanted to belong to him.

Only him.

How *dare* he ask me to show him what I want?

Gritting my teeth, I lifted my eyes. He sensed my defiance, and I enjoyed the brief flicker of surprise on his beautiful face. "No," I said flatly. "I'm not begging for anything. Not anymore."

Seth's lips twitched at the edges. I expected him to frown, but his languid smile sent trembles into my heart. "You still have some fight in you. Good."

Hooking the rope between my thighs, he pulled it, ground it roughly against my engorged nub. It should have hurt, I wished it had.

Pleasure swelled in me, my pussy clenching around nothing, my belly fluttering with a nearby orgasm.

He'd taken me to the edge so quick. So easily.

My defiance meant nothing.

Chuckling, he reached around, cupping my ass. We were bent together like a pair of dancers, his breath on my temple. "Go on, keep denying it. Try not to come like the helpless slave you are. You'll never hold out. Your body belongs to *me*, Ms. Starling. You're mine... every part of you."

Perhaps I was really losing it, because I thought there was a sense of desperation in his voice. The way his breath hitched, quickening... it wasn't the flat, ultimate calm I knew him for.

The flogger was back, he spanked me with it as he cradled me to his chest. The strikes were brisk, but they never lingered. Each one made me flex against him, driving the ropes deeper, pushing the flames in my core higher.

His cock was solid against my thigh, its presence adding to my fervor.

The fibers in my back ached, my calves knotting from how I strained. Every noise I made was a whimper, or a throaty groan. Seth really did know me; what I wanted, what I needed...

He knew it better than *I* did.

Wriggling in my bonds, the immense pressure of my orgasm began to mount. It was a tidal wave, roaring through me with every tiny twitch of my body. The ropes trapped my clit, grinding it over and over.

Redness flushed across my chest; I started to shake. Seth squeezed my jaw, making me look forward—right at the mirror. "Watch yourself," he whispered. "I want you to see how amazing you look when you give in."

My lashes flickered, but I didn't close my eyes.

I wanted to—I thought I wanted to.

I didn't know anymore.

Seth had turned me into a blank slate that had simple, basic needs.

The flogger came down one more time, caressing my tingling ass. The final arch of my hips doomed me.

"Aah!" I gasped, my lips numb, hanging open. Furious heat slammed into me. My muscles tightened as I came. In my ear, Seth moaned. He was relishing how I'd lost control, coming in the bondage he'd crafted for me.

Waves of pleasure turned me pink. In the mirror, I saw my slack jaw, the sparkles in my eyes. I writhed obscenely, my inner thighs shiny from my release. It was humiliating, but also... so much more.

Seth wasn't wrong. When I looked at myself like this, there was a beauty to it. A celebration of trust. I'd let him do all of this to me. I'd agreed to it from the start.

The reward for such obedience was humbling.

"Perfect," he purred. "You're so god damn perfect."

I couldn't talk. The ropes were still digging into me, never letting up. They didn't care that I'd just come; they had me in their grasp, and they were unrelenting. "Help," I whispered pitifully as a new wave of hot pleasure strangled me. "Fuck, take them off, I can't... I..."

"Can't what? Handle more?" Laughing, he kissed my cheek. "I think you can. I've seen it."

Blood pounded in my ears. The room swam, and I rolled my hips like a stripper on a stage. I was coming again before I could prepare, the ropes forcing me without caring what I wanted.

Sobbing, I threw my head back. "Fuck! I—this—aah!" Colors blurred, I was a wet, convulsing mess. My world centered in on my pussy, the heat there burning through my consciousness.

 could do nothing but come, even when I was sure it was too much.

Then, with one final, blurry look at my reflection...

I felt nothing more.

- Chapter Seventeen -
Naomi

Blackness choked me under.

It had arrived suddenly, stealing all sensation from me as I floated along. I only realized I'd passed out when I saw I was sitting naked on the floor.

Confused, I lifted my head, my returning senses telling me how sore I was. Around me, there was warmth; a pair of arms, holding me against a solid chest. Seth's forehead rested on the side of my skull, his legs stretching on either side of me.

"Seth?" I asked, shaking the cotton from my brain.

"Naomi. I'm... sorry."

I was sure I'd heard him wrong. Not just the apology.

He'd called me Naomi.

Not Ms. Starling.

Not even Opal.

What had happened while I was unconscious?

His presence was smothering me; I was slick with old sweat and in no state to make sense of anything. Twisting, I tried to get him to look me in the eye. "You're sorry for what, punishing me?"

Seth met my stare, turmoil in his rich blue irises. "No. I loved every moment of that."

Hugging myself, I grazed a mild mark across my chest from the ropes. It would fade, I could tell he'd tied me up with care. *If he isn't apologizing for doing this, then...* I needed to understand what he was trying to say. "What do you have to be sorry for?"

"Days ago," he said gently. "Upstairs, the night I lashed out and banished you. I'm sorry for all of that."

Am I dreaming? Or just going nuts? "You don't need to apologize. It made sense for you to be so angry." Finally given a chance to explain everything, I pushed on. "But what I did was an accident! I never meant to cause so much trouble."

"It was no accident. What you did was deliberate. Breaking the rules, going through that door... You changed everything." He adjusted me in his lap. His eyes were as molten as silver, coating my soul.

I shivered violently. "You told me I almost *ruined* everything."

Scowling, he shook his head side to side. "I was a fool, scared of losing the world I'd built for myself. Furious that I was falling for a woman who could expose me entirely."

Falling for me.

The rest of his tirade sank in. "I wouldn't!" Leaning up, my forehead touched his chin. "I would never tell anyone what goes on down here, Seth. I really wouldn't. All of it... it means everything to me, too."

It's true. My body was pulsating. Everything was pulsating. *Becoming Opal, it gave me an opportunity at a new life. A new existence.*

And I want it back.

Hesitating, studying the curve of his mouth, I dropped my voice. "*You* mean everything to me, Master Onyx."

Saying that name was like invoking a demon.

Crushing his lips to mine, he shoved me against the floor. Seth trapped me, held me in place so he could remind me of all the things about him that I needed.

The kiss was long, it had my lungs screaming. When he finally pulled away, air was rasping through his clenched teeth. The gleam in his eyes, I knew it was reflected in mine. "You mean that, don't you?" he whispered.

"Of course, I could never lie to you!"

His smile was indulgent, it soon became a sneer. "No. You couldn't."

Seth lacked the slow, cool collection he'd wielded in the past. Here, with my feelings so naked, he was ravenous.

His fingers clawed into my hair, capturing me securely. Teeth clamped on my earlobe, then rubbed down my silky throat. Everything he did made me groan, everything he was drove me wild.

Scrabbling to hold onto his back, I knew my brain was turning into pudding.

Pushing his chest against mine, Seth breathed in my scent. Hearing his greedy moan, it had my eyes rolling in my skull.

My hair was a tangle, falling across my breasts. I reached out, wanting to undo his shirt buttons. Instead, he straddled me and sat up, doing the job himself.

I didn't mind. He was much better, much more quick, than I would have been.

Seth crouched, rubbing his smooth chest over mine. I was still so sensitive from earlier, his minuscule movements had me whimpering.

Wrapping his lips around one firm nipple, he suckled me, my knees grinding together. Each tug at my breast made the walls of my pussy thrum, like they were connected by invisible threads.

He pet my areola, lazy circles that made me breathe faster. "Your body is so easy to read," he whispered. Blowing cool air on the slickness of my damp nipple, he chuckled at my sharp gasp. "I love it, really."

He... loves it?

Hooking his arms around my thighs, Seth lifted me until my ass was in the air, my slit inches from his lips. Staring straight into my face, he inhaled my scent loudly. Seeing the lust cross his expression, it cranked my arousal.

Running his tongue over my swollen lips, the man lapped at me like he was parched for water. Each stroke made me cry out, my fingers digging into the floor.

Soft lips circled my pulsing clit, embracing it in luscious pleasure. I was sure I couldn't take any more. My flesh was tender from the bondage.

When he suddenly dipped his elegant fingers deep into my clenching tunnel, he showed me he knew better. Wriggling inside of me, Seth held me tight as I gyrated with wild passion.

My cunt rippled over his thrusting fingers. His face, when he smiled at me, was drenched. *Oh god, my heart might explode!*

The wetness was audible, his fingers slipping free. For a moment, I felt the aching pain of emptiness. Seth was fast, removing his belt and pants without issue.

Leaning down, he kissed me roughly. I tasted my own sweetness on his tongue. The plump tip of his cock was warm, the only warning he was about to shove himself deep into my eager pussy.

I braced myself, vibrating with desire for him to fill me.

Seth brushed his nose to mine, speaking soft, insistent. "Do you need me to fuck you?"

"I—yes, of course!" I was having trouble focusing.

"Then," he said, bending to whisper into my ear, "I need you to do something for me."

My mouth was dry, sticky. "Anything, just tell me!"

"Agree to be mine." His cock slid along my slippery lips. "Agree to come back, to finish the mural... and to never break my rules again." The more he talked, the greater my pussy ached. "Or, my sweet Opal, I will not fuck you. I will not give you the cock you so desperately need. What will it be?"

I looked at him squarely, my lips smiling upwards at one corner. I could see the confusion welling in his gaze. He needed an answer. "That's all? You didn't need to bribe me to get that. It's what I wanted all along, Master Onyx."

His consternation melted, transformed into a thing of gluttony. Holding my shoulders, he pressed me into the floor, driving his entire length into me in one fierce stroke.

It was the answer we had both wanted.

I squealed, thrusting to meet him. The sound of our carnal dance filled the room, wet and desperate. His teeth found my throat, my nails dug into his sides. Whatever sharpness the pain delivered was muted by the delightful throes of heat rising in our centers.

I'm so close, so god damn close.

My insides were grasping at his swelling cock, locking him in place. But I wasn't strong enough to hold him. Tensing, the pressure mounting to a peak, I groaned openly while the orgasm took control.

Inside, I felt him thickening. Above, his breathing was heavy with exertion. *He's going to come, too!* Realizing how near his release was, my desire soared. *Is he going to do it inside of me?*

He hadn't before, but it would be hard for him to pull out in time.

Roiling with anticipation, hot with a taboo desire, I wrapped my thighs around his lower back. If he'd debated yanking free, my position made it impossible.

Burying himself to the hilt, Seth grunted into the crook of my neck. His skin was white-fire, his cock thickening.

Rivulets of his essence poured inside my hungry pussy. It set me off again, the orgasm slamming into me, stealing my breath. Each

254

muscle was a single spasm that never seemed to end.

What gift did this man have, that he could always give me such pure bliss?

Together we laid there, panting on the soaked floor.

Lifting his head, Seth watched me, a finger trailing my collar bone. "Did you mean for me to finish inside of you?"

My grin was sly. "In the heat of everything, it just felt right."

Wrinkling his brow, Seth chuckled. "You really do love risks."

I couldn't deny that. Everything that had drawn me to Seth had been risky.

"When you agreed to be mine," he asked. "You meant that?"

His question stunned me. How could he even wonder about my sincerity?

Crushing my lips to his for a short second, I snuggled closer. "Of course I meant it. I meant every word. I'm yours, Seth. Master Onyx. Whatever you want me to call you, I don't care. I... I love you," I admitted.

Seth froze, his stare unmoving, targeting me.

My face went tomato red. *Why did I say that? What if he doesn't...*

Those thoughts became ash as he rolled

me on top of him, still buried deep inside of me. His kiss could have stolen the last breath from my lungs, left me a husk, and I wouldn't have minded. "Naomi, I love you, too. I never thought I would say those words, but I mean them."

Radiant, I said no more, only wanting to taste his mouth. The mouth that had been both cruel and kind, the mouth that had banished me...

The mouth that had brought me home.

I'm his. Truly his.

I desired nothing more.

- Chapter Eighteen -
Seth

I stood in the shadows, my hands folded at my waist.

Though I'd watched many slaves get collared, I'd never performed the act myself. There were candles on stands, gentle music, and people lined up in rows patiently. It reminded me of a twisted wedding, but that imagery had me smiling.

"I still don't know why you're doing this," Helm whispered beside me. "I've never seen you collar anyone. Why now, and why her, of all people?"

His bitterness wasn't surprising. Helm had a taste for rebellion, and I knew he'd seen the same fire in Naomi that I had. Unlike me, though, he wanted to snuff her flames out. Few Masters were as fierce as him.

I'd have banned him from my club, but the girls never complained. If they didn't mind has rough touch, who was I to judge?

No, I mused, thinking about how forceful I'd been with Naomi. *I have no place judging him. I'm not much better.*

The broad man was watching me, his mouth curled. He wanted a response. Sighing, I smoothed the front of my outfit. I was wearing a silver vest, the tie an emerald green over my charcoal shirt.

It was as close as I would come to embracing the real me, and my Master persona, in one setting.

"Why am I doing this?" I asked, tasting the question. "I suppose she left an impression on me." Shooting him a sly smile, I chuckled. "Are you hoping to change my mind, buy her from me in a grand gesture?"

Scowling, Helm walked away. "She's all yours."

Yes.

She was.

The room was packed. Masters stood against the walls, every pair of eyes focused on the curtains. They wanted to watch the ceremony, either nostalgic for when they'd claimed their own girls, or eager for the opportunity to get their own later.

Slaves, kneeling in quietly, were thinking of similar things; the time they'd been collared, bought by a Master so they knew where they belonged.

The uncollared girls were envious, wishing for such a gift.

A hush sank across the gathering. Expectantly, I watched the curtains. At first, nothing happened. The excitement was palatable, made worse as the moment stretched.

What is she doing? Did she get cold feet?

No. I knew how much she wanted this.

Finally, Naomi appeared.

Everyone else would recognize her as Opal. But, for me, she would always be Naomi. We'd lifted away our secrets, revealed to each other who we really were.

In more ways than one.

Naomi was wearing a long, flowing black dress that clung to every delicious curve. It rolled down her arms and over her hands like long gloves. The fabric hid all of her skin, save for her head...

And her elegant throat.

In her white mask, she turned my way. The smile she flashed me was genuine. Hell, I don't think she could hold it back.

This was what she craved. *It's funny,* I thought. *I banished her for trying to force me into doing this.*

Now, it was hard to picture my future without this woman.

She swayed my way, hips kicking with flirtatious desire. Instantly, reminded of how her ass felt in my hands, my cock thickened in my briefs. *Damn tease.* "Opal," I said, once she was within a few feet of me. "You understand what is about to happen to you?"

Holding her chin up, she looked regal—then she wavered. I could tell what was wrong; she wanted to be proud of this moment. However, acting cocky wasn't ideal for a submissive.

Hanging her head, she said softly, "Yes, Master. I understand entirely."

Nodding, I turned towards Helm. He handed me a small box, the cherry-wood shining in the candles. It was beautiful, but it would pale when compared to the contents.

Taking it from him, I opened the cover slowly. Inside, white pearls, opals, and diamonds glimmered in beautiful serenity. There were a few murmurs in the crowd, and I heard Naomi muffle a gasp.

The collar cost a fortune. Anyone could see that.

It would glimmer like a chandelier in the sun., drawing every eye around. I *wanted* the world to see this woman was wearing my mark. For them to take one look at the expensive piece and understand that she was worthy of such a gift.

Honestly, she was worth far more.

"Kneel," I said firmly. Naomi bent down, folding with the agility I'd seen in her when she painted. Amazement still glowed in her eyes.

She'd expected something subtle, easy to hide.

I would never let her hide.

Lowering the collar, I swept her hair aside. The metal wrapped around her pale skin, the lock clicking loudly—pointedly—into place. It wasn't impossible to remove, but I had the only key. Naomi would always wear it, unless I said otherwise.

I didn't imagine myself every letting her take it off.

My fingers brushed her ear, then cupped her chin. In the shadows, her eyes were imploring. "You now belong to me. *Only* me. Body, mind, and soul... you are mine."

She trembled; it went through her whole body. "I'm yours. Forever and always."

Her swaying curves had gotten me hard earlier. The words she spoke now... well.

Nothing had ever turned me on so much.

Smiling, I helped Naomi to her feet. Bending near, I whispered, "The collar looks very fitting on you."

Around us, people clapped. It was a polite noise, reverent. Under the buzzing hum, Naomi took a quick breath. "Can I tell you something secret?" she asked softly, so no one could hear.

"Yes. Always."

She reached up, brushing the expensive surface of the collar. "Nothing has ever felt so right."

My heart thumped, and I went silent. *She means that.*

How had I gone so long, avoiding a moment like this? What had made me run from collaring a slave?

Staring over Naomi, taking in her proud smile, her glittering eyes... I realized what had held me back.

None of the others were like her.

Naomi was special; more so than I'd even guessed.

I'd fought the urge to claim my own sub until now, because none of them had been right for me.

I loved this woman.

God, I actually loved her.

Reaching down, I clasped her hand. It wasn't a normal gesture for a Dom, and I sensed how she stood straighter at the touch. But I didn't fucking care. Not anymore.

Even if this whole club crumbled... if my world was ruined, my secrets exposed...

I had Naomi.

And that was all I would ever need.

- Epilogue -
Naomi

I set the last of my things inside the cardboard box, hoisting it in my arms tightly. Seth had told me he'd send people to help me move, but I'd insisted I could do it myself.

I own so little, it only took me a few hours to pack.

Kicking my door open, I caught my reflection in the window. The image made me halt.

Even in the foggy surface, the glittering, jeweled collar was magnificent. The day Seth had locked it on me... it was one I'd never forget.

But, if I had, this over the top symbol of possession would remind me.

I'd explored it once I was alone. The smooth stones felt good under my fingers. The clasp was securely locked, a thing that thrilled me in a funny way. Seth owned me, and even if strangers didn't quite understand what that meant, they still had a suspicion when we strolled around together.

Perhaps they thought it was a gift from a husband to his wife.

Or that Seth is a sugar daddy.

Snorting, I carried the container down my steps. I was planning to bring it to the front, for when Corbin arrived. Out of the corner of my eye, something caught my attention.

The flag for my mailbox was up.

I thought I changed my address already?

Setting down the square burden, I opened the tiny metal door. A collection of papers spun to the ground. Groaning, I bent to gather them up, shaking my head in irritation. *I won't have to deal with this anymore at Seth's place. Corbin probably brings the mail to him by hand.*

Thinking about the fact that Seth had asked me to move in with him made me smile. It had been an offer I couldn't turn down.

Besides, in a way, I'd been mostly living in his mansion for some time already.

Of course, I don't look forward to explaining this to Mom. She'd think I was nuts, or maybe she'd get a bit of greed in her once she heard how rich Seth Hart was.

Rolling my eyes, I straightened out the pile. It looked like everything was junk.

Everything but one envelope.

It had that official sort of crispness. I recognized the name on it instantly.

Dropping everything, not caring where it

fluttered, I tore the envelope open. With shaking fingers, I unfolded the paper, reading the familiar words. Only, this time, what was written at the very bottom was not some cold rejection.

Seth had been right. His letter would do the trick.

I'd been accepted to the California College of Art and Design.

****

The scent of paint was strong in my nose, my mind bent to my work. I didn't hear him, didn't sense him, until he wrapped his arms around my waist from behind. Warm lips touched my neck, his chuckle muffling my pleased gasp.

"Seth," I laughed, placing my paintbrush on the pallet. "You surprised me."

"Don't I always?" he mused, spinning me so he could taste my lips. Falling into his touch, my brain melted like candy in the sun. Releasing me, he stepped back so I could see his pleased smile. "That painting is coming along nicely."

I stared up at the wall. It was one of the many stretches of white in his home—my home —that I'd been eager to get to work on. "You like it?"

"I do, very much." Reaching out, he pulled me against him so we could stand and view the mural in comfortable silence. "What does it mean, what's its story?"

I gazed over the scene wistfully. It was almost entirely black, curling like fog that consumed everything. There, in the very center, was a white bird flying proudly. On its chest was a golden heart.

It would have been easy to assume the darkness was chasing the bird, harming it, but I knew better.

In such a short time, Seth and I had become incredibly close. He'd been my boss, my secret lover, my enemy, and then my Master.

We'd fought...

We'd fucked.

There had been nothing that wasn't hot and wild between us, good or bad.

I'd wanted to capture the soul of our existence. I didn't think the painting did it true justice, but how did you capture such powerful emotions in a mural?

Still...

I'd tried.

"It's a story about love, and not fighting it when it comes calling," I said pensively.

Seth nuzzled my cheek, stroking my

throat around the collar until I whimpered. "So it's a story about us."

"Yes," I agreed, proud he'd understood. "It's a story about us."

Pressing his lips to mine, Seth smiled around our kiss. The wall held me up, his shadow blocking out everything but the fire in his stare. "I'm looking forward to our next chapter, little jewel."

"Yes," I said softly, touching the collar I wore with pride. "I am, too."

This wonderful man wanted a future with me. We didn't need masks. We didn't need secrets.

In this confusing world, no matter how broken or damaged...

No matter what monsters hid inside our minds...

We loved each other.

And that was enough.

THE END

~ABOUT THE AUTHOR~

A USA Today Bestselling Author, Nora Flite loves to write dark romance (especially the dramatic, gritty kind!) Her favorite bad boys are the ones with tattoos, the intense alpha types that make you sweat and beg for more!

Inspired by the complicated events and wild experiences of her own life, she wants to share those stories with her audience.

Born in the tiniest state, coming from what was essentially dirt, she's learned to embrace and appreciate every opportunity the world gives her.

She's also, possibly, addicted to coffee and sushi.

Not at the same time, of course.

Check out her website, www.NoraFlite.com, also email her at noraflite@gmail.com if you want to say hello! Hearing from fans is the best!

-Nora Flite

Check out more of Nora's books!

The Body Rock Series:

Hard Body Rock

She thought she was stepping into fame:

Meeting Drezden Halifax should have been a dream. But dreams are supposed to be sweet, fragile things that whisk you away. Not monsters crafted from hard fingers, gritty vocal cords and a voice so powerful it could tear my guts right out.

Maybe my heart, too.

Becoming the guitarist for Four and a Half Headstones was everything I needed.
Too bad the band's lead singer is doing his best to ruin everything I am.

He thought she would solve his troubles:

Lola Cooper, god damn Lola Cooper. She was the perfect guitarist, fingers that could summon a sweet song or punch a chord. She's supposed to save my band, make us come out of this tour in one piece...

But I just want to tear HER to pieces.

No one should make me feel this way. One look at her, one smell, and I knew I'd have to have her. She does things to me that scare the shit out of me. Make me want to slam her on a wall and listen to her cries: eager or fearful, it doesn't matter.

I'm a monster...
And I don't even care.

Genre: New Adult Rockstar Romance
This is the first installment of the Body Rock Series
25,000 words

Slow Body Rock

He knew he was addicted:

I thought it'd be smoking that killed me. Lola is
more addictive than tobacco could hope to be.
After feeling her warm body, touching her
skin... even if it was an accident, I've given up.

The monster inside of me is going to consume
her.

I'm too tired to fight it.

And I honestly don't want to.

She knew it was risking everything:

Why is he trying to mess up my ONE
opportunity at success?
My very god damn existence?
I can't handle this pull between us... a gravity
that wants to knot our bodies together and
leave me merged.

Ruined.

I thought Drezden cared about his band, that
he wouldn't dare do anything that might break
them— and me— apart.

When did I become the one thing worth losing
it all over?

Genre: New Adult Rockstar Romance
This is the second installment of the Body Rock
Series
25,000 words

Flawed Body Rock

She wanted to be a rockstar:

I finally have everything.
Fame, presence, the world knows who I am.
Now my life is even harder.

What do you do when every eye watching you is
full of jealous hate?
I'm strong enough to not let strangers hurt
me...
But when it's my own brother, the stakes
change entirely.

He just wanted her to himself:

My claws are in her, but I'm trapped, too.
Waking up, my first thoughts used to be about
music.
Lola's changed all of that.

She consumes my dreams; my existence.

My band... the girl I'm obsessed with...
Is there room in this world for both of them?
If not, which do I choose?

Genre: New Adult Rockstar Romance
*This is the third installment of the Body Rock
Series*
25,000 words

True Body Rock

He never wanted to look back:

I've always run from my past. It's what keeps me sane; whole.
But what if not facing it means losing the girl I love?

Telling her the truth must sound so simple.

It's a request that could leave me more broken —more hollow and wrecked—than ever before.

She never saw it coming:

Answers.

Answers answers god damn answers.

How far do I have to go to find out what I need? To get to the bottom of the filth and finally find the real person waiting? The man behind those delicious green eyes and intoxicating lips?

If Drezden won't talk to me...
I'll find someone who will.

But why does it feel like they're the one who's been waiting for me?

Genre: New Adult Rockstar Romance
This is the fourth and final installment of the
Body Rock Series
29,000 words

Stand Alone Novels:

Only Pretend

If you hated your life—wanted to prove to the world that you could change—how would you do it?

I had a plan. I also had no family, no friends, and definitely no jerk of an ex-boyfriend who thought I was boring.
I was tired of being me.
In Vegas, I could be anything.

And then I saw him.
His hungry smile wanted a taste of the new me.

Only a boring person would have said no.

It was reckless to follow a stranger to his bed. Dangerous to take the drink he handed me. I thought the worst regret I'd have would be a hangover, a walk of shame through the hotel.

Except I didn't wake up in the hotel.
Or in Vegas.

I doubt my face will end up in the news. "Woman missing," the headline would say. "A stupid person who thought she could be someone else."

I'm not someone else. I was only playing pretend.

Too bad he was playing for keeps.

—Author's Note— This is a dark romance novel, it contains themes of violence and mature situations that could make readers uncomfortable.

Watch Me Fall

Pain, abuse, brutality. That was my life. I struggled and stressed; cried until I forgot what tears were. But I worked hard. I clawed to the peak.
And then I lost everything.
Most people would have shattered.
I'm not most people.
My dreams are gone, but that's fine. I could have lived this tiny, broken life. I could have suffered in silence.
Until I met her: Noel.
God, she's so alive. She makes me ACHE and I just...
I can't ignore her.
So I won't.
Noel thinks she can handle me. Survive me.
If she knew the truth—could see into my mind —she'd smarten up and run.
I'm so lucky she doesn't have a clue.

—Author's Note— This novel is a stand alone. It contains scorching sex, violent themes, and mature situations that could make readers uncomfortable.

Last of the Bad Boys

All I've ever been good at is fighting and fucking.

Pure violence and wet sex. For years, it's been my life. If you think I'd get bored, you'd be very wrong. I'll never get enough.
Nothing can sate the ache that wants to bend any and every woman over, just to see how she tastes. I'm a man who aims to please, but no one holds my attention.

No one but Zoe.

I throb at the very IDEA of her... I want to suffocate with my tongue inside her thighs.
When my phone rang, I didn't expect her pretty voice to beg me for help.
She thought I'd save her and that'd be it. Well. Too bad.
I'm hooked on this girl—I want her more than water or air.
I wasn't her first.
But I planned to be her last.

Author's Note-- Standalone full-length novel. Contains explicit and erotic scenes, a dirty bad boy with a filthy mouth, as well as themes of violence/mature situations.

Exposing the Bad Boy

Adrenaline is my drug, and nothing has ever rivaled my addiction.
Not until now...
Not until Ellie Cutter.

That cinnamon smell intoxicates me, her lips were made for bruising. You'd think she'd jump my bones like all the others, but she's all business; so calm and collected.
That just makes me want to see her melt under my touch even more.

I've tasted the bodies and curves of so many women. Ellie shouldn't have any affect me.

So why can't I stop thinking about that one damn kiss?

It meant nothing... but the memory could make my zipper tear in two. I keep waking with my hand under the sheets, every bit of me hot and heavy.
It's madness. Illogical. Reckless.

The only cure is to make her mine.

Author's Note-- Standalone full-length novel. No cliffhangers!

Outlaw Road

Ronin

I've always made bold moves. What can I say?
Life gets too easy.
But when that poker game ended... I didn't
expect to win myself a gorgeous girl.
She's wild, determined, and clearly has a death
wish. My kind of lady.
Too bad she hates everything about me.

Flora

I was supposed to save my sister.
No matter how hard I tried, I still failed. Now
I've been kidnapped by the same men.
After being used and hurt by bikers, I never
expected one to help me.
But I still don't trust him.
He's as bad as the rest of them... So why does
he keep protecting me?

*Outlaw Road is a full length stand alone MC
Romance novel. Contains a sexy biker with a
filthy mouth, extreme tattoos, and just the
right amount of danger. No cliffhangers here!*